Other Books by
E. H. Clark

DEATH PAD
VINDICATION

Coming Soon

UNKNOWN ALLIANCE
VIPER 1

Chapter 1

The business climate at Canon Aeronautics had changed over the past two years. The remote-controlled airplane manufacturer had branched out with a large military contract. Michael Canon had started the company with twenty employees and now had two plants and over three hundred good people working two shifts. The company's state of the art security was handled by Michael's long time friend R. C. Billups. It was not only a standard security organization, it was also a secret on call mercenary detail that had been drawn into several do or die situations over the years. It wasn't originally planned that way, it just happened. His plant in the cities manufactured their standard line of remote-controlled boats, cars, and standard sized airplanes. The newly acquired plant in Salt Lake would build two different styled planes. The Army had originally contracted for twenty of the one quarter scale Giant Corsairs and F-15's and had just bought twenty more of each. Business wise it was a dream come true.

Michael wasn't as fortunate in his personal life though. A few years earlier his wife, son and daughter were tragically killed. A drug cartel had inserted a deadly drug and a team of mercenaries in his city. He and his special security team eliminated them. Over a year later another group appeared in two other cities. In an unusual turn of events, Michael and his team were secretly asked, by members of a law enforcement agency, to help them rid their cities of a Colombian cartel's hit team. They cautiously took on the task and played out their magic once again. Each time he lost good men only to have new people come into his life.

He began a new life with Andrea Lane only to have her leave because of his inability to let someone else save the world. It had been nearly four months since Andrea left for the east coast to try and put her life together. They had a non-interference pact between themselves and Michael honored it. Having been sidelined in a battle only several months earlier with a brain aneurism, Michael had begun a non-stop fitness program for himself. He worked out for two hours every morning before work in the company's fitness facilities, and after a full day of business he worked out for one more hour. Those close to him admired his drive but a few worried he was taking physical fitness too far too fast. Something or someone had to break him out of this peril or his life would change for the worse.

As he sat down behind his desk his secretary, Marsha, brought him two messages. He looked at one and laid it by the phone. The second one was from a D.R. Marshall MD. He read Renee's message, pulled a side drawer open, and put it on top of a stack of other messages sent by her. He had no plans to return her calls. He was keeping them as a reminder of what they signified.

R.C. came in and poured them both some coffee.

"I know I shouldn't say this Michael, but I am worried about this routine and pace you're keeping. The doctors told you to go easy on yourself."

"I know Richard, but I can't seem to keep focused. I still think about Andrea."

"Monica hasn't heard from her in several weeks but we assume she's safe and working like she said."

"It's been tough not being able to even call her," Michael said sipping his coffee.

"It's only been a few months. She might change her mind."

"I really don't think she will. Deep down we both know that. Therefore, I've made the decision to move on. I have to come back to the living."

"I wasn't going to say it but Monica doesn't feel she will come back either."

"Anyway, what do you hear from the guys?"

"Well, Stacy won her last racing event with C.J. at her side. What a pair they make. I think half the team is now helping Stacy in some manner. Scott and Victor are doing great and the guys that helped us from Seattle are…"

As R.C. rattled on, Michael's thoughts went to C.J. and his long time friendship with Tamara. Tamara had saved Michael's life. In doing so she became disfigured. What bothered Michael was C.J. breaking away from her as he did. Since she had nobody, Michael took Tamara under his wing and sent her to plastic surgeons in San Francisco.

"And that's about it. What do you hear from Tamara?"

"She's doing well. I'm flying down to the bay area on Friday to see one of our vendors. If there is time I'm going to try and see her."

"Give her our best. Boy, was that gal something," R.C. said as he turned and left.

Michael picked up the message by his phone and dialed the number for the Thunderbird housing complex sales office. He had mentioned to the sales department that he might sell his home if the price was right. He paid one hundred eighty thousand for it. With the executive park now full, they felt they could sell it for two hundred sixty thousand dollars easy. Several buyers were interested.

Earliest sale might be within thirty days. He told them to proceed with selling it.

He finished the day and skipped his workout routine. He stopped by the florist and picked up some flowers. He had set aside time each week to go to the cemetery. After placing the flowers into the permanent vases on each headstone he sat down on the ground between them. He looked at the marble markers for Susanne, Jennifer, and Christopher Canon. Thoughts of them as a loving family only a few years earlier would mix into his mind. He smiled at things they did but then his thoughts would take a downturn. He had not been able to protect them and now they were here. This was the one thing in his life he could come to grips with. After thirty minutes he said his goodbyes and headed home.

He had the people in shipping put some boxes in his car just in case his home was sold soon. After fixing something light for dinner he began to pack away things he wouldn't need right away. A lot of things he came across made him wonder why he ever kept them in the first place. They wound up in the garbage or stacked neatly for the VA. With two boxes sealed he started on the third box. He opened the bottom drawers of the dresser and came across one item that sent mixed emotions through him. Sitting down on the bed he rubbed his hand across it then put it to his face. With his fingertips he felt the soft silky material. He smiled as thoughts of how the Redskin jersey had put unimaginable excitement into his life and Andrea's. Mental flashbacks brought smiles to his face while his eyes started to water. He laid it back down where he found it and slowly closed the drawer.

Chapter 2

As the business week continued Michael seemed to be losing interest in his work. Meetings, though very important and needed, were becoming boring. He found himself paying visits to all of his employees throughout the day. His momentary visits meant a lot to the people but Michael was searching for something he couldn't find.

Early Friday morning, whether it was fate or luck, the message flag appeared on his computer monitor. He smiled when he opened the email.

Hello Michael,

I have missed talking with you. I am so glad you sent me here to the Bay area. It's so beautiful. I am doing well with my surgeries. On a different note, you did promise to come and visit me. I know it's only been only six months but is there a chance you could come down anytime soon? By the way, C.J. never did buy me that dinner. If you remember, you said you would make it good. I'm going to hold you to that. Anyway, just thought I'd drop you a line and maybe brighten your day as you have mine for caring.
Fondly, Tamara

He sat back, smiled, and sipped his coffee. "Well, I did tell her I would, why not?" he thought.

Hi Tamara,

I guess a promise is a promise. Why don't you make reservations around seven tonight at your favorite

restaurant and we'll make the promise come true. I'll call you when I get in.
Sincerely, Michael

The Falcon left the city at eleven and touched down at the Oakland airport within the hour. Mason and Kennedy accompanied Michael to his meeting with their vendor. The meeting was over by four and the three headed to their motel. Mason, Kennedy, his plane crew Ernie, Jeff, and Molly were going to a Raider's game at seven and would meet Michael in the morning. Michael showered and called Tamara. She was excited and gave him her address. He got a taxi and headed across the Bay Bridge.

The forty minute trip in the beginning rush hour traffic seemed like an eternity before Michael finally arrived. As he walked into the lobby of the Sheridan he could see her coming towards him in a half walk, half run cantor. Her smile could have lit up the darkest night. He held his arms out and she practically went through him as they held each other for a moment then kissed.

"Oh Michael you don't know how good it is to see you."

"Let me look at you. You've let your hair grow. I like it."

"It hides some of my features, but I'm glad you approve."

She took his arm and they walked to the elevator. She hugged him once more before the elevator stopped on the twelfth floor and the door opened.

"I had looked at a lot of apartments and finally decided to stay here. I told them I was going to San Francisco State University and had been in an auto accident.

I told them I just needed a place to stay and they gave me a super rate," she said as she opened the door marked 1212.

As he looked at the one bedroom suite he smiled at her ingenuity. She opened the drapes to the patio and he followed her out. The view was spectacular. She stood at the railing and pointed out some of the historical landmarks. He acknowledged them but couldn't take his eyes off her. Several of the knife scars on her face and forehead area were barely visible. The doctors were doing a fantastic job with the plastic surgery.

She was about five foot nine inches tall and concealed her shapely figure well in loose fitting clothes. She was wearing blue jeans, white boat deck sneakers, and a shirt that fell below her waist. Her hair was down on her shoulders and she had let her fingernails grow. This wasn't the fierce warrior he had sent here. He put his arm around her and her head found his shoulder. They looked out at the ocean in the distance. He kissed her hair and she squeezed his side in acknowledgement.

"Why don't you fix a drink and I'll get ready," she said as they headed back inside.

He broke up some ice and fixed a Bacardi and Coke. He heard the shower run for several minutes then shut off. The sound made small tingles of excitement go through him. He knew he couldn't allow this to take his mind over so he turned on the TV. It wasn't so much the news he liked, it was the commercials and the various marketing techniques they employed.

"Are you really hungry?" Tamara said from the bathroom.

"It's been a long time since I had lunch on the plane. How about you?"

"I'm starved. I think you'll like the place I picked out. It's not far from here."

He turned the TV off then relaxed to the sounds of her in the other room.

"I'm ready if you are," he heard turning his head to the left.

She was wearing a three-quarter length black evening dress and three-inch black high heels. He stood up and smiled with approval as she walked to him. Her eyes sparkled and she knew she had his full attention. He held his arms out. He held her for a few seconds then she kissed him gently as not to smear her lipstick.

"I so want to please you Michael. Is this too much?"

"No not in the least. Is this the same young woman I sent to the big city months ago?"

She smiled at his question.

"Do you have something for your shoulders? It can get pretty chilly here at night."

"Just this sweater. I didn't bring much when I came here and I haven't wanted to buy many clothes yet."

"You aren't by any chance carrying your arsenal of weapons are you?" Michael grinned, as he put the sweater over her shoulders.

"I might have two or three on me but you'll have to search me to find out."

"Are you tempting me?" Michael asked as he opened the door.

"Maybe," she said as she squeezed his arm.

They took a taxi for the ride to the restaurant. As they neared the site Michael asked the driver to pull over and stop.

"Let's go in here for a minute," Michael said as he paid the driver.

They walked into Fashions by Elaine, a boutique for all tastes. Tamara was very wide eyed as she let her fingers slide along all the silk and satin racks of clothes they passed. Michael told the woman that approached them that they wanted to see some evening jackets or coats. She led them to the rear of the shop. Several young women modeled items the saleswoman thought would be appropriate for casual eveningwear like the one Tamara adorned. From experience Michael would look at the modeled item then quickly glance at Tamara to see her expression. It wasn't long before a three-quarter length coat in leather was modeled and Tamara's eyes lit up. The woman saw Michael nod his head and she had Tamara put the red coat on. Tamara looked dazzling in it and yearned for Michael's approval. He smiled and said they'd take it. Just before the woman removed the tags for her to wear it out, Tamara took Michael aside.

"Oh Michael, I can't get that. Did you see the price? Nine hundred dollars. Maybe we should go somewhere else."

"Do you like it?"

"Oh yes, I love it. It is so soft and comfortable."

"Then we'll get it. I can't picture you in anything else," he said as he handed the woman cash.

The woman put her sweater in a bag as Michael put the coat over her shoulders. He saw her eyes close at the feel of the material.

She held his arm the half block they walked to the restaurant. She thanked him over and over. She didn't want to check it at the cloakroom, but Michael just smiled and helped her off with it. The atmosphere was one of casual quinine and semi-disco. He mentioned to her he never was into fast dancing and she understood. She just wanted to be with him but stated a slower dance might be in the offering later. They ordered a drink at the same time they selected dinner.

"I understand it's getting close to your next birthday. Do you have a list of things you might like to have?" Michael asked.

"The dreaded thirty-two, I don't know if I can stand it."

As dinner was served, Michael smiled as he looked across the table at Tamara. He didn't lie to her when he said how beautiful she was when he mentioned it in Salt Lake. He could see a different Tamara than everybody else saw and felt good about her accepting his help. As he looked at her physical features he wanted to be even closer to her than across the table. He thought about him being almost twenty years older than she was. He also couldn't accept that as being a factor. She put her hand on his. She had always hid her feminine features for her own reasons but tonight he pleasured in the slightly low cut evening dress she had picked out especially for this occasion. As they finished eating she asked of Andrea.

"I feel funny asking you this but do I remind you of her?"

"No not at all. I do cherish fond memories of her and me, but tonight is special to you and me. I don't think of her when I look at you if that's what you're wondering."

"I'm sorry Michael," she said as she put both her hands on his. "I didn't know how to ask that."

He raised her hands up and kissed them. She felt a little better. The waiter came over and Michael ordered a carafe of coffee. They could hear music faintly in the background.

The establishment had two dance halls, one at opposite sides of the main dining room. They walked to the disco studio first. Michael put his hand by his ear as the sound reverberated through his head. He asked her something but she couldn't hear him as people kept bumping into her on their way to the standing room only dance floor. He felt her pulling his hand. It wasn't to the dance floor, it was back out towards their dining room corridor.

"I can't believe I used to get caught up in that, maybe I've grown out of it," Tamara said as they walked to the other dance area.

They stood for one song and watched a dozen couples move and embrace to the music.

"I love this song. Want to give it a try?" she asked.

He led her to the dance floor and stopped. At full arm length he pulled her back into him as the DJ played *The Last Farewell.* He couldn't believe how good she felt in his arms and they moved slowly together as one. She kissed his neck and he pulled her a little closer to him. He wanted to squeeze her tighter but fought the urge. The song was fitting as they danced slower than the others around them. They waited for one more song hoping they wouldn't be disappointed. They weren't as *Love Me with All of Your Heart* played. Had they control of the turntable they would have played it again and again. As the song came to an end, they went back to their table.

"Thank you Michael, that was so beautiful."

"Yes it was," he smiled.

They finished their coffee and left.

* * * * * * * * * * * * * * * * * * * *

The cool night air typified the evening weather in San Francisco as the slight chill always had a touch of romance in it. They took a taxi back to the Sheridan. She kept rubbing her coat and he could tell from her expressions how much it meant to her.

In the apartment she turned on several small sidelights and he hung up their coats.

"How long can you stay Michael?"

"This is your day and I'm your captive audience."

They walked out on the patio and absorbed the city's lights for about ten minutes then went back in. She fixed some coffee for them and they enjoyed it over inquiring conversation about the two of them. She slid over the half a cushion distance between them and he put his arm around her.

"Michael, your arm feels good. I remember you holding me in the hospital. I've thought about sitting there with you with the blanket on our shoulders. Oh, do you remember the nurse? She didn't want us to be there together. I think you scared her."

They laughed. When she turned up to look at him he put his hand on her face and kissed her softly. She turned into him putting both her hands around his neck. He let his lips slip from hers and kissed her eyes. She put her head by his neck.

"Michael, that was so nice. I knew it would be like that."

He turned her slightly and she moved onto his lap.

"Better?"

"Yes, very."

She felt good in his arms. He kissed just the way she hoped he would and tested him often.

"I think I am really wrinkling this dress. Maybe we should take a break and I'll find something not so tight fitting?"

"Like a little more coffee?" Michael asked, as she left for the bedroom.

"Just a half a cup, thank you."

A minute went by and Tamara called for him.

"Can you help me with this zipper? I thought I would never get it up when I put it on."

She slipped out of her heels and turned her back to him. He fumbled with the very stubborn clasp for nearly a minute. It finally released and he slid it slowly down her back. He held her shoulders and kissed her neck softly from one side to the other. He kissed the middle of her silky soft back. He could see several scars she still adorned from her encounter. She moaned quietly as she could feel the dress wanting to slide down.

"Undress me Michael," she said softly, which sent twinges of excitement through him.

He let the dress slide down below her legs and she stepped out of it, throwing it on the bed. She hadn't turned around which excited Michael even more. He put his hands on her hips. She pulled his hands around to her stomach and then up to her breasts. She squeezed his hands into them and uttered sounds of pleasure as she bent her head back next to his. He felt her body shudder as if a cool breeze had gone by. In a few moments she turned to face him but never pulled away far enough for him to see her full body. She held him then kissed him hard on the lips. She unbuttoned his shirt and pulled it open allowing her breasts to absorb his warmth.

"Oh God Michael, stop me if you must but do it now if you're going to."

He kissed her hair and slipped out of his loafers without looking down. She unbuckled his belt, opened his slacks and let her hands move them down to the floor. He finished undressing as she held him tightly. He kissed her eyes then her lips softly as he moved slowly down to her breasts. Sounds of pleasure were emitted and he could feel the electricity shoot through her body. His lips and tongue surrounded every inch of her beautiful firm mounds as she held his head and guided him slowly where she wanted him to go. His hands found her panties which he slid down off her hips. He kissed her stomach and felt her pubic hair on his chest and neck. He stood up and held her against him, her nails digging into his back. He placed his hands on hers to let her know she was squeezing too hard. She relaxed her fingers then brought one of her hands down to his erection. She moaned her satisfaction as she raised it between them then slowly pushed her lower body into his to feel what she wanted so badly.

"It's been a very long time since I've been with someone Michael. Let's take it slow."

"Let me get a towel," he said as he turned and went into the bathroom.

The only thought he had was he wanted this now more than ever. He reentered the bedroom to see her standing next to the bed looking at him coming towards her. Her body was strong and so shapely he wanted to devour every inch of her. His own rigorous exercise routine had hardened and toned his body to one of someone her own age. She stopped him about arm's length from her and he threw the towel at the foot of the bed. She let her hands move from his muscular chest to his stomach allowing her fingers to run along the lines of his well-pronounced stomach muscles.

"I fantasized but never imagined how beautiful you were," she said as she kneeled in front of him, sliding one hand down on his left hip, the other on him. He placed his hands on her head lightly as she began to kiss his stomach and caress him. He could feel stronger and stronger sensations as she carefully and gently engulfed him, wanting every part of him to be hers. He bent lower and put his hands on her shoulders as the sensations were beginning to mount to a point he couldn't control unless he stopped her. She sensed this and came up slowly kissing his stomach, chest, and then ending at his lips.

His hand guided her to the middle of the bed. He looked at her as she lay there. Her breasts were so pronounced, her stomach visually soft and flat. Her pubic hair was nicely trimmed and very full. He started kissing her right thigh and worked his way up to her right breast. She rose up and kissed him hard on the lips several times muttering words of passion, which only excited him further. He started down at the same pace he had come up the other side, sliding his hand along her stomach and through her hair. He could tell by her movements she was ready to explode but wanted to test her own limits. Ending at her thigh he started back up between both legs. He knew she couldn't take much more foreplay. She brought her legs up and spread them slightly as he neared the tepid zone. His tongue was the fuse that caused her back to arch and her fingers to rip into the sheets as she screamed out repeatedly. He had to use all his strength to stay where he was, to stoke the fire he had lit. Her legs nearly crushed him as she wildly endured a second orgasm.

They were both very wet now as she soon pulled him up to her and kissed him repeatedly. She reached down between his legs and set his swollen member up to the place she now wanted him. As he entered she grasped his waist and began drawing him in. Moans of delight came out as he slid deeper and fuller into her. He wasn't in all the way when she stopped his forward movement to signify she was at her end. He moved back slightly and began a rhythm with his hips that created another orgasm to explode from within her. Her legs squeezed so tightly he felt heavy pain around his waist and hips. He grimaced and remained where he was. When he again reached her limit of entry she now pulled him into her and yelled out from the pain. He said he didn't want to hurt her like that but she insisted she wanted all of him, whatever it took. Another dozen entries allowed him deeper and it seemed she had put the pain out of her mind as she worked his hips stronger with her legs and heels. He could feel himself getting larger as the ultimate feeling was about to happen within him. She also sensed his rapture approaching and timed her own to his movements. He climaxed as his last stroke went in as deep as he could now go. She screamed and climaxed with him. She wouldn't allow him to slide back as she held him firm with her legs and arms. She could feel him repeatedly pulsate strongly within her which only escalated her own juices to flow. It was over a minute before each could feel the muscles of the other begin to relax. He kissed her eyes and entire face and neck. She rubbed his body the extent her hands could reach. He rolled to his side and she stayed right with him. Their breathing became calm again as she ran her fingers over his face. He kissed them as they touched his lips. Soon they took a hot shower together. The renewed touch of their hands exploring each other's bodies allowed them to start the night all over again.

"You know it's three thirty?" she said as she lay on his arm.

"Want to go until dawn?"

"Oh Michael, I can't move now, I mean, I will if you want to."

Michael smiled and kissed her. He knew he couldn't go another round with her. He was surprised he had enough left for the second time.

"I've only imagined what this could be like Michael."

"If you could have picked one night in time to experience the inner you, then tonight was that night. You were so receptive I couldn't get enough of you."

"Will there be other nights like tonight for us?"

"We can only wait and see what happens. I would like to think there will be."

She was lying nude on her left side with her arm under her head on the pillow. He let his hand slide along her arm and moved it softly against her nipples and breasts. He continued along her stomach and her lower area. His touch caused her breathing to become softer as she had nothing left. She fell into a deep peaceful sleep. He gently rolled her over on her back and brought her arm down, covering her in a sheet. He fell off to sleep without any worries the world outside had to offer.

* *

Michael could barely open his eyes as he got out of bed and went to the bathroom. He put some warm water on his face with a washcloth and then looked at himself in the mirror. His reflection gave a new meaning to the word exhaustion. His body ached and his lower rib cage and sides felt bruised. He smiled as the reason for its destruction entered his mind. He wrapped a bath towel around himself. Walking to the hall he stopped to look back at Tamara lying quietly in bed. He made some coffee and poured two cups. He stopped back in the bathroom and put hot water on the washcloth then grabbed a towel. Putting the coffee down on the nightstand he sat on the edge of the bed.

"Is that coffee I smell?"

"Could be, see for yourself."

He pulled the sheet down and she put her hands on her eyes to keep the light out. "Michael, I must look a fright, please don't look."

"You look beautiful to me," he said placing the now warm cloth in her hands.

She laid it on her face and eyes for a few minutes and thanked him, as she dried her face with the towel. He bent down and kissed her. She had no problem with that. They sipped their coffee and thoughts of the night flashed through her head.

"Last night was so great Michael. I had a wonderful time going to dinner and picking out my new coat. Thank you. I'm going to pay you back for it. What time do you have to leave?"

"It's eight thirty now and we're scheduled to fly out at eleven. I should leave by ten. How about some breakfast?"

"Right now I have to use the little girl's room," she said as she started to get out of bed. He put her robe around her shoulders but she could barely walk.

"Damn Michael what did you did to me? I can't move."

He smiled as he helped her to the bathroom door. He poured them some more coffee. He had his slacks on by the time she came out and was standing at the patio doors looking out. Her robe opened as she put her arms around him and laid her head on the back of his neck. He could feel her warm breasts against his back and tingles of excitement began to dart through him again. She stood there slowly moving her hands on his chest. In a moment he set his coffee on the side table. Turning to her he opened her robe a little wider and pulled her to him. They kissed and he held her a minute.

"If yesterday was my day, when does the day end?" she asked.

"That's up to you. I still have over an hour before I have to leave. Do you have any suggestions?"

They took a long shower together and made the remainder of the hour very slow and easy.

There were no promises made or anything else for them to look forward to. She wanted it that way and he would live with her wishes.

The taxi took an hour to get to the airport where the team waited. Once in the air Michael had Molly bring him four aspirin with his coffee and breakfast.

"How was your evening? How was Tamara?" Mason asked.

"She's doing well, but it will be a few more months before she feels she can come back. She was hurt pretty bad. As for our date, I don't know how she had the energy to dine and dance the entire night. I think the damp night air did me in. How was the game?"

They practically gave Michael a play by play of the entire game with the Raiders winning with twenty seconds to play. They thanked him numerous times for the tickets and the great seat locations. He closed his eyes and let his mind go back through his own evening with Tamara. They landed within the hour.

Chapter 3

Michael skipped his daily workout routine, as he needed at least another day for his body to find order. After two meetings he sat in his office and looked at the results from the Army testing. He looked up as his email flag sounded its tone.

Good Morning Michael,

You can't know how much having you here meant to me and I know you feel the same. After you left I laid back down and felt all the places you touched. I could still feel you there and fell back to sleep thinking of everything we did. Anyway, like I said, I am scheduled to be here for several more months and I'm hoping you can come down again over that time. It would mean a lot to me but, if you can't I understand. You be well and think of me from time to time. I will know it when you do.

My Love, Tamara

He sat back and reread the message. He could feel a spot being made in his heart for her and it gave him a warm feeling. As he sipped his coffee, his thought pattern changed as a mental kaleidoscope of thoughts began to flood his head with flashbacks of happenings, both positive and negative over the last several years. He leaned forward, elbows on his desk and put his head in his hands. He felt like a migraine was coming on. He could never put Tamara in harm's way again, he thought, and having her with him could surely bring that to fruition. He had no answers for anything the future might ask of him. His thoughts were interrupted when R.C. came into the room.

"We have big trouble at Fort Collins," he said handing Michael a communiqué that had just come in.

Michael read it and laid it down on his desk. "What do they expect using a live ammo run on personnel. Who in the hell authorized that?"

"I made a call and I'm guessing Major Hawthorne gave the word. Live ammo was put in by mistake instead of the paint rounds. At least nobody was killed."

"No but three soldiers are in the hospital shot full of holes. I think Billings gave the word. Hawthorne takes his orders directly from him. I guess we're going to have to get out there. Tell Robbins and Boston we'll pick them up on the way there."

"There's a Colonel Billings on line one, Mr. Canon," Marsha said on the speaker.

"Thank you Marsha. Colonel, I was expecting your call."

"I figured you were. I feared this might happen and you have a lot of explaining to do. We are suspending these operations until a board of inquiry convenes. I would like you to be here at ten o'clock tomorrow."

"We'll be there. I'll send a list of personnel I am bringing with me and..." Michael tried to say when he heard Billings hang up.

"He's not a happy camper. Get everything ready. We're out of here at four AM."

Michael sat there and pondered the situation. His eyes glanced back to his computer monitor and a smile broke out on his face.

Hi my beautiful Tamara,

I share the same thoughts as you and couldn't have put them more eloquently than you did. Being with you did mean a lot to me, and yes, there is a good chance I will be coming back down before you're out of there. We're having a problem with the Army and will be flying to Colorado in the morning. Wish us luck. You keep focused on getting well and it won't be long before I will be down to see you. I will be thinking of you too.

With Love, Michael

He sent the email, then had Marsha set up a conference call meeting to the Salt Lake group. The meeting lasted over an hour, as a list had to be made of any and all things that could have gone wrong on our end. Max Post explained to them what they might expect from the meeting at Fort Collins, to prepare them mentally. The Salt Lake team would work on it the remainder of the day. They would pick them up at seven AM.

Chapter 4

It was raining when the Challenger 6 touched down at Fort Collins. Three cars and a security detail met them as they deplaned. Captain Briggs was the ranking officer. Michael, R.C., and Grant Robbins rode with him back to the base. They received visitor's badges and followed Briggs into a large meeting room. After meeting with the flight team in charge of flying the Corsairs they asked to see the planes and the ammunition. They were taken to a hangar area where all the planes were stored. Michael's team began an investigation into the mishap. They worked hard for over two hours then requested a meeting with those heading up the project. Several boxes of ammunition were also to be brought to the meeting.

The meeting time was set at two o'clock. Two Army sergeants had been assigned to them while they were there. At eleven thirty they broke for the noon meal.

To several in the team it was like old home week as Mason commented that nothing had changed since he was at a base like this in the 80s. The food was very good and nothing was left on their trays.

They arrived at the meeting room at just before two and took their seats. In front of them was a raised table with five chairs which quickly were filled with five officers. One of them was Colonel Billings.

"Good afternoon Mr. Canon. We'd like to thank you and your team for coming to this pre-inquiry hearing," Billings began. "I understand you have conducted your own investigation and we would like to hear what you've found."

"Colonel Billings, gentlemen, thank you for letting us be a part of this investigation," Michael began. "As our contract with the Army clearly states, Canon Aeronautics will supply all aircraft, spare parts, and training needed to facilitate compliance with the contract. We have conducted a full inspection and several things have stood out that we need to discuss."

"Our inspection teams have also looked into this and they report everything points to vendor packaging errors. What do you find differently?" Billings asked.

"We are not here to point fingers at anyone, Colonel, but I would like to bring something to the attention of the panel here today," Michael stated, as he had R.C. open the lids on four ammunition boxes that sat on the table before them.

"Ammunition in box number one here is exactly like we ship to the base. As you can see it is clearly marked LIQUID AMMUNITION. There is red seal tape across the opening to the rounds with the word, Liquid marked in yellow letters."

R.C. pulled the tape back exposing the red tipped paint target rounds then laid it on its side facing the panel of men.

"Box number two is clearly marked LIVE AMMUNITION .19 CALIBER. Blue seal tape is across the opening with LIVE ROUNDS written in yellow letters."

R.C. repeated his first procedure.

"These two boxes we brought with us today. The Master Sergeant here was kind enough to bring us these two boxes kept in your armory. Both ammunition boxes are painted Army colors, which one would expect."

R.C. picked a canister from the box and faced it toward the panel.

"Not only was the box painted Army colors so were the canisters including the tape across the opening."

R.C. repeated the procedure on a canister in the fourth box.

"Now, I would ask you which is the live round canister and which contains the painted rounds? The answer is this. Box number three here is labeled live rounds and box number four is labeled liquid rounds. If I may ask one of you on the panel to come down and remove either of the brown tape across the canister, I think you will find something interesting."

"Master Sergeant Hammer, remove the tape from them one at a time," Billings ordered.

Hammer walked over to the first questionable canister and removed the tape. All could clearly see the red tips of the bullets in the canister. He repeated the unveiling showing the fourth canister had live .19 caliber rounds within.

Two of the officers at the table came down for a closer look. They now understood the dilemma. They returned to their seats.

"What you are saying, Mr. Canon? Is all the ammo we have now worthless because we can't be sure which are live and which are practice rounds?"

"Not exactly. As you will notice when any canister is inserted into the wing of the plane it has to be turned sideways ninety degrees. It is clearly marked, as on this one, LIQUID. On this one, LIVE. This is pointed out when we train the personnel who handle the planes. I understand the morning the planes were armed it was dark and raining.

In haste to complete the task, this observation, we conclude, was overlooked. We've done it ourselves but caught it as we double-check everything before we test. I would like to make two suggestions to the panel. First, that the seal tape across the canisters remain unpainted. As mentioned in our original contract negations, we offered to paint the Army colors before shipping. This was not included in the contract. I would like to again recommend this procedure be initiated at Canon Aero. As far as the ammunition already painted we would be glad to inspect the entire ordinance already sent, and put the appropriate tape markings on them."

Michael sat down as the panel talked between them. For several minutes the entire room remained silent.

"Mr. Canon, we thank you and your team. We accept your offer of replacing the seal tape. I will initiate the necessary steps to have you do the painting in your facilities. We would also like to extend our thanks and appreciation in your handling of the situation. We further feel this was an oversight on our part therefore, you're company will be properly compensated for your additional work. I feel we have taken the appropriate steps to see this cannot happen in the future. This inquiry is concluded."

Members of the panel came down and shook hands with Michael and his team, then looked at the boxes of ammunition.

"Colonel, I am sorry to hear about the men that were wounded. How are they coming along?" Michael asked.

"Just fine, thank you. I have to admit those planes of yours are nothing short of lethal. We've used them on some other projects. I've got to tell you they can tear up some terrain."

“Thank you Colonel. I’m glad we were able to work together to solve this problem. I will have a team here tomorrow to start work on the seal taping as you suggested.”

Michael and his team were driven back to the Challenger 6, and they were cleared to leave.

“Michael, I swear to God you are the best I’ve ever seen,” Post said as Molly brought him some Ginger Ale. “You had them wrapped tighter than a tourniquet. They had absolutely no place to go.”

“I want to thank all of you for a job well done. A special thanks to Grant Robbins who found the discrepancy in the first place.”

They all applauded each other. Molly brought Michael four aspirin. Michael sipped his hot tea then sat back to lose some of the inner tension he built up during the investigation. They were very lucky this time to find the answer to the problem this quickly and he knew it.

Chapter 5

During the next three weeks following the hearing at Fort Collins, Michael worked closely with his Army project R & D team in Salt Lake to initiate still another safe guard in the aircrafts firing system. R.C. could see the long hours were starting to take a toll on Michael.

"Monica and I are barbequing later. What do you say you come on by and tip one with us."

"Are you doing the cooking?" Michael asked as he sat back in his chair.

"Why of course. You don't think I put that in your inexperienced hands do you," R.C. said with a laugh.

"If you promise to burn me at least three wieners then I'll come."

"You made my day. I'll tell Monica," R.C. said as he left.

Michael's afternoon was spent in two meetings that took most of the day. He cut his workout to only an hour.

"Hi gorgeous," Michael said, as he put two pies down that he picked up at a bakery. He gave Monica a kiss.

"Where's mine?" Stacy asked as she wiped her hands on a towel.

"Right here," Michael said giving her a quick kiss on the lips.

"That Stacy is such a little sweetheart," Monica commented, as they watched her take a plastic tablecloth outside.

"She's my little tomboy in disguise. By the way, where is what's his name?"

"You're terrible, Michael."

"You know I only think of you and nobody else," Michael smiled as he opened the refrigerator and grabbed two beers.

Monica popped him on the butt as he walked out to the backyard.

"Hi Boss."

"Hey Mason, Shawn, where's the old man?"

"Just follow the smoke."

Just then a large billow of black smoke rounded the corner of the house.

"I'm thinking it's a lot safer taking on a drug cartel than rounding the corner to see where that smoke is coming from," Michael commented.

They laughed and followed Michael. R.C. was swinging away with a handful of paper plates trying to push the smoke away from the grill.

"Here, hold these," Michael said as he handed R.C. the beers.

Michael pulled the grill off the small concrete slab and out into the yard about thirty feet. The smoke stopped swirling and rose straight up.

"I was just about ready to do that but you didn't give me a chance," R.C. said as he threw Michael one of the beers.

"Just watch where the wind is blowing. You know it swirls around the corners of the house?" Michael said with a smile.

"Hey, I was barbequing long before I met you. You keep that up and I might just have to whip your ass before this day is out."

Laughter erupted from the guys leaning against the fence out of the smoke's way. They joined the others.

"R.C. you stop talking like that to our guests," Monica said as she and Stacy put some bowls on the picnic table.

"I might just start with her," R.C. said with a wink to Michael as he turned the hamburgers.

"Well then bring it on Shorty. The last time you tried that you couldn't walk for three days," Monica grinned then walked into the house.

Arron and C.J. fell to their knees then back flat on the lawn laughing so hard.

Kennedy put his hand on his side when it hurt from laughing. "You know I think she could do it too."

"OK, you all just keep it up and you're in big trouble," R.C. said with a smile.

Michael knew that R.C. purposely started talk like that to break the atmosphere at all outings if they got stagnant. Monica was very quick witted and lived to jump in on him, which made it even better.

"Excuse me, Shorty. Could you pass me..." Mason tried to say then lost it.

R.C. grabbed a handful of potato chips. Monica smiled and yelled "Hey" as she pointed her finger at R.C. Now everyone's stomach was sore from laughing. They all dug in and enjoyed the great barbeque spread. Compliments were given big time to Monica and Stacy on their picnic. R.C. got some credit for his part. That was always the case in a comical way. When it was all over everyone pitched in and cleared the table.

"Monica, everything was great," Michael said as he put a stack of dirty plates in the sink. "You're so good for Richard. He really lucked out having you."

"Yes, I like what we have. I am so glad he has you and the guys around him. He lives for that."

She was loading the dishwasher then stopped when Michael asked, "What do you hear from Andrea?"

She dried her hands off and put her arms around him.

"Michael, I'm so sorry. It wasn't supposed to happen like this. I heard from her yesterday and she is fine. She has met someone in Washington D.C. He's some kind of a Senator, or diplomat, or someone like that. I don't know where it might go."

"Hey, that's all right. I'm very happy for her. I've learned to live with it. I cherish the memories we had together. She has a life too. Give her my love and all my best the next time you talk to her, will you?"

"I will. Michael you are so wonderful," she said as she wiped her eyes.

Michael rinsed his coffee cup, refilled it, then went back outside.

R.C. was in a foursome playing horseshoes. The other guys were just lounging around enjoying a beer. He sat down on the grass then leaned back on his right arm to watch.

"When are you coming to the races again Boss?" Stacy asked, as she sat on the grass next to Michael. "Did you hear I won another race?"

"Yes, and congratulations. I also heard you have two new Rangers."

"You can't believe how lucky I've been since the day I met you. I was down to nothing and now I could buy a racing team and sit back and watch them drive."

"I heard you talking about our encounter in Utah. Have you recovered from Salt Lake yet?" Michael asked.

"That was an experience I'll never forget. It happened so fast I never had time to really think of what the outcome could have been," Stacy answered. "Can I ask you a personal question? You don't have to answer if you don't feel comfortable."

"Sure, anything."

"I was afraid for Tamara with Barco. I still relive some of it. Is it only me or do some of the others have problems with it?"

"No, we all do in our own ways. That's why we plan it so closely to try and keep the unknown factors from jumping up. I still think about our first encounter with the cartel, I always will. But we're all safe now and that's what's important."

"I was so afraid for you that night Michael."

"You were?"

"Yes. You weren't well. I've always worried about you when we go out."

"I thank you for that."

"Michael, do you think I have a split personality?"

"Why would you say that?" Michael questioned.

"I don't know exactly. When I'm with the team my mind changes into all business and my senses go to a level I never knew they could. Then when I race my truck the mode changes into a free spirit with nothing to lose. Right now I haven't a care in the world."

"No sweetheart, your problem is you need a boyfriend."

"Yeah right, a boyfriend. My busy lifestyle doesn't allow for that."

"Oh it doesn't, does it?" he said as he tickled her. She laughed out loud.

"I heard you stopped by and saw Tamara. How's she doing?"

"Her surgeries are going well. She hasn't decided whether she's coming back or not."

"Michael, when she took on Barco, she wouldn't let me shoot him. Everything happened so fast."

"You would have done what had to be done. It was personal with her. She was protecting you, Jim, and me from him. As expert as he was with a knife, he couldn't have beaten her."

"I still relive that night," Stacy said with a wrinkled brow.

"I hope that it will all pass in time. What do you say we see what's for dessert," Michael said as he extended his hand and helped her up.

The party lasted another hour then it broke up. Michael went home, took a shower then called it a night.

Chapter 6

Michael had just finished signing all the review sheets the department heads had given him earlier in the week on all the employees. He had given a five to nine percent raise to the entire workforce. He was way ahead of his projected earnings schedule for the year, and he owed it all to them. Just then a thought came into his mind and he turned on his computer.

Dear Ms. Garrett,

I've been thinking about going out for snow crab legs. I understand Fisherman's Wharf, near you, has some good ones. My problem is I don't know anyone that might share my passion for seafood. Let me know if you know of anyone interested in joining me.
Mr. Canon
PS I miss you

It was an hour before he heard a chime from his computer.

Hello Mr. Canon,

I have searched high and wide but have had very little success trying to find someone to help you with your dilemma. You being a stranger to the area, may I suggest me being your guide to the Wharf?
Your local guide for hire, Ms. Garrett
PS Ditto

Michael laughed out loud.

Dear local guide for hire,

How about meeting me at the World Airways Jetport around ten tomorrow morning? Take a taxi and I'll rent a car.

Fondly, Michael

He sat back, lit a cigarette then sipped some coffee. He heard the chime.

Oh Michael, do you really mean it, you're coming down? I won't sleep a wink tonight. I really do miss you and can't wait to show you how much. Until tomorrow

Lovingly, Tamara

The Falcon touched down at nine forty-five and taxied to the assigned slip within World Airways Jetport. The crew longed for a weekend in the Bay Area so them finding something to do was no problem. As Michael walked down the steps of the Falcon he saw Tamara looking through the windows of the small terminal. He waved back at her and went up the steps. The sight of her standing there smiling nervously waiting made him want to run to her but he kept his composure. As he entered into the terminal she came up to him. He opened his arms and she filled the void.

"Oh my darling, I thought this moment would never get here," she said as she kissed him a second time.

"Do all guides greet their clients like this?"

She lightly bit his lip. He laughed and she took his arm.

Michael rented a Lincoln and they drove out of the airport. He told her all about what had happened with the

Army and she was all ears. Anything about Michael she absorbed and wanted more. Within the hour they parked on the Wharf and they slipped their windbreakers on.

"Do you know we're wearing the same colors?"

"Did you call somebody back home and ask what I was wearing?"

"No silly, I think it's beautiful. Everybody will know we're together," Tamara said as she took his arm.

They walked along the long row of landmark fishing boats, stopping occasionally to talk about the ones that caught their eye. Commercialism had certainly fallen on Fisherman's Wharf as the shop owners tried to get them to come in and shop around by giving out discount slips. They just had fun with all of it and kept walking until they reached the food plaza. They accepted several of the free samples being given out. Michael watched her and absorbed all the excitement she was radiating. The sun overhead made her ash blonde hair glimmer and sparkle. He wasn't nearing fifty; he was in his thirties again. They sat down at one of the umbrella shaded sidewalk tables. A large seafood variety platter was served along with two small umbrella drinks that looked good on the menu. They sampled everything and lavished at the goings on around them.

"Michael, I'm so glad you're here. I needed this break."

"I know it's tough on you. How is everything going?"

"Now it seems we have good days and some of the others. We are about to begin the final phase where they're redoing the deeper incisions. The doctors are so good. I know this is costing you a fortune, at least let me help with the finances."

"No, I won't even think about it. The insurance is taking care of eighty percent of it, and I've got the rest. How is your side wound?"

"It's fine, well, when it gets really damp out I feel some discomfort, but that's all right."

"I thought I might have hurt you when we were together last."

She smiled. "That was a wonderful hurt and not the injury, just everything else. I thought I wasn't going to be able to walk straight again."

They laughed at the thought.

The afternoon was spent going through many of the shops. Michael was always fascinated with the wave making machines that adorned the windows of one of the shops. They stood with their arms around each other and watched as one of the ten-foot long wave models slowly generated its cascading flood of simplicity. It was almost hypnotizing. They walked from one end of the Wharf to the other and even had a professional picture of them taken. By seven they decided to have dinner at one of the premier restaurants. They had made inquires and chose the consensus.

The atmosphere was warm and romantic with a lit fireplace just a few feet from them. They looked out on the water and saw boats slowly making their way effortlessly through the full moon's path. She loved to look at him as he talked. He was so important to her. For the first time in her life she knew she had finally found somebody she could truly, and without question, love. His company and financial independence meant nothing to her. She just wanted to be near him and do everything with him. At times she could sense he was feeling the same way towards her. Enjoying him physically, even to hold his arm as they walked while they were together was enough. When he was far away she had him deeply embedded in her mind and heart. If that was the way it had to be then she would accept it.

They both had the Alaskan snow crab dinner and he ordered her favorite wine. He looked at her, as the flickering rays of firelight accentuated her profile.

"You are so beautiful Tamara," Michael said, as he put his hand on hers. "How could I be so fortunate to have found you?"

She squeezed his hand and smiled. "But you did, and I'm glad."

"You look so tired, do you want to skip dancing all night and go home?" Michael asked as they finished their coffee.

"I don't know how I've lasted this long. I hope it doesn't show that much."

He smiled. "My body is telling me to find a nice place to land too."

He paid the check and they left.

* *

The Wharf was crowded with people as they made their way to the car. They were back at the Sheridan inside of twenty minutes.

She again turned on only the sidelights in the room as they entered. He went into the bathroom as she unlocked the patio door, and then slid it open. He came out and found her looking out at the beautiful night. Putting his arms around her he held her tightly.

"My darling, why is it when you hold me it's like my life is starting all over again."

"Maybe it is and this is only a preview of all your lives to come. If my memory serves me correctly they do call you "Cat."

He felt her suppress a laugh, then squeezed his arm. The chill was now becoming evident as she turned around and kissed him.

"Keep me warm tonight," she said and kissed him again.

He was only in the shower for a minute when she joined him. She soaped her hands then rubbed them over his shoulders gently, feeling the muscle contours that played out. His back to her, she brought her arms under his chest and stomach. Her soapy hands slid gently from his chest and downward. He turned and faced her. She loved his touch, even more so when he turned her around. She closed her eyes as he purposely slowed down his movements as he caressed her backside. She had felt tingles of excitement when he did her back and buttocks but now she turned her back to him. The sensations were beginning to build as his hands moved ever so slowly from her breasts to her stomach then inched lower. She backed into him tightly as his fingers started to rhythmically massage her. She moved her legs apart a little more and she gripped onto his arms as he was now caressing the one vulnerable spot for which she had no defense. He moved his left hand and arm under her breasts to steady her as he could feel her body beginning to constrict as he moved his fingers to match her impulses. She said his name several times as her body tightened. She gripped his forearm tighter. Her orgasm seemed to take every last ounce of strength from her. She momentarily put her hand on his to stop his steady circular massage, then aided him in the same manner as another round of waves shot through her. He helped her up from her slightly bent over state and held her to him.

"My God Michael, we've got to shower alone."

"Whatever you say."

"I'm saying don't listen to what I'm saying."

He laughed as he handed her a towel.

Approaching the bed, he looked at her as she lay on her stomach. He got into bed and kissed her shoulder.

"My darling, I think you better get some rest. You've had a long day. I think I'll just lie here and watch you sleep."

Michael smiled and agreed with her as he pulled the sheet over both of them. He kissed her and turned out the lights. He smiled to himself as her breathing quickly went to a soft easy rhythm. In an instant she was void of any other movement.

Chapter 7

Michael woke around six and followed his usual morning routine. He made some strong coffee and took two cups into the bedroom. She was lying on her stomach with the sheet at her waist. He sat down and just looked at her for a minute. He reached down and moved a strand of hair off her cheek. A smile began to form on her lips.

"Come on you faker, open those eyes. A new day started hours ago," Michael said as he sipped his coffee.

Her hand covered her mouth as he could see the big smile coming out. "Damn where do you get your energy?"

"From trying to keep up with wild women who keep me up late. Want some coffee?"

She laughed as she pulled up the sheet, then sat up.

"Why are you so good to me?"

"Cause I think you're cute?"

"No I'm not. You said I'm beautiful. Don't you remember?"

He smiled as he put his arm around her. She nestled in close and put her head on his shoulder. They finished their coffee and he set her cup on the nightstand. Her eyes were closed as he held her. She began rubbing his chest and stomach slowly with her right hand. She let her hand drop lower and lower.

"Don't start anything you can't finish."

She smiled and pulled him on top of her back across the bed. He began kissing her stomach then her breasts. Her fingers ran through his hair as he moved up on her.

"I love this body," she said as she placed him gently. He caressed her breasts as she began to slowly move on him. He watched her eyes close as she engulfed him with everything she had. She only lasted about ten minutes before collapsing from utter exhaustion. He ran his hand along her wet body.

"Michael, if just for this moment, tell me you love me."

He kissed her very softly then told her he did. She pulled him to her and held him very tightly for several minutes.

At Michael's sly suggestion, they would waylay their showering until they got back from breakfast.

They found a home-style breakfast place and talked about work and flashbacks of the cartel's failed attempt to get a foothold in the US. It was turning out to be one of San Francisco's typical beautiful days as they drove towards the Golden Gate Bridge.

As they approached the bridge they took the Presidio exit and climbed the streets to the top. They parked in the State park's tourist lot and then walked up the hill. To their right was the majestic bridge, the true gateway to the Pacific. Straight ahead of them was the Pacific Ocean. They held each other as they watched the waves come ashore far below them. Other couples walked past them, enjoying the same sights. Following the cliff south they finally got down to the beach. They now walked barefoot on the cold wet sand to the even colder water. They laughed at how tough they were as warriors, but let the icy chill of the water get the best of them. Soon they sat on some driftwood and put their shoes back on.

"I would give anything to make love to you right here," Tamara said.

"The thought had crossed my mind," Michael said as he pulled her up. "You're recuperating from surgery and your doctor said that you weren't allowed to do that."

"No he didn't. You're making that up," she said as he started running down the beach.

He let her catch him then laughed as they wrestled. The rest of the afternoon was spent going up to the fort and just enjoying their time together.

They started back to the Sheridan and he was momentarily lost. He pulled over and stopped. They could see where they wanted to go, which was below them, so decided to take a left at the next street. Just as he did the front of the Lincoln went down sharply and he slammed on the brakes.

"Damn, I always wanted to know where this was. What a time to find it," he said as they looked at the sign next to them which read: LOMBARD Street. They started down slowly and not a word was uttered by either until they got to the end.

"You will never find a more crooked street than that my darling," Michael said as she continued to look back.

"Wow," she uttered. "Stacy would have loved that ride."

They went back to the Sheridan and relaxed awhile before dinner.

"Do you really have to leave in the morning?"

"Yes, the plane has some maintenance to be done tomorrow afternoon."

"Well why don't you let them take the plane back and you have them pick you up here on Monday or better yet next Thursday?" she suggested with a big smile.

She curled up into him on the sofa.

"Boy, you're no longer the little cat. You've turned into a tiger."

"Well you started it."

"Me, what did I do?"

"Well for starters you've brought out things in me I thought weren't possible."

"Like what?"

"Well, you keep making my legs so weak and I may never walk again. I'll need you to stay here and take care of me," she tried to say with a straight face then started laughing.

"What do you do when I'm not here? Have you found another boyfriend?"

"No silly, I know how to put things totally out of my mind. Come on, make my knees weak again."

"Haven't you had enough yet?"

"No and I want more and more. Even if I have to sit in a wheelchair the rest of my life it'll be worth it."

He laughed and tickled her. She crawled all over him and to make her stop he agreed to letting her have one more before dinner. Her place of choice was right there on the sofa. Unlike before it was both of them that now couldn't move. They laughed about it.

They decided to order dinner in, as they were both too tired and sore to go out. After dinner they watched a movie on the TV. She lay on his arm after he turned out the light by the bed.

"Have you given any thought about what you might do?" Michael asked.

"I've thought about it from time to time and I think I'm trying to justify everything that has happened, especially now with you. I think in the next couple of weeks I should know."

"You know I'm always there for you in whatever you decide. I asked you to go through so much…"

She put her fingers to his lips. "I did it because I wanted to and you needed me. You kept me close so I wouldn't get hurt and little did we know, we both almost lost everything."

"Things are now starting to pull together at Aero and maybe I can free up some more time for us to do more things."

"Michael, you know that I love you more than life itself and you just knowing that is all I ask."

She rolled over and kissed him. Soon they both fell asleep.

* * * * * * * * * * * * * * * * * * * *

"Morning Boss." Kennedy said handing Michael a newspaper as he boarded the plane. "Good weekend?"

"Yes, I had a very good time sightseeing, how about you guys?"

The Falcon took off and Michael listened for about ten minutes to the teams exploits in the big city. Molly brought him four aspirin and some hot tea. He settled in to read some of the paper on the trip back.

Chapter 8

The next several months went by quickly, amidst the meetings and testing of new aircraft components. Tamara spent a lot of time sharing her martial arts skills at a local Asian temple. The one constant thought on Michael's mind was Tamara. After his first meeting on Thursday he turned on his computer and smiled as he typed.

My Beautiful Tamara,
Do you realize it's nearing a year since you left here? Knowing what a sheltered life you must be leading I was wondering if you would like to get out of that stuffy high-rise you live in. Maybe a trip down the coast is what you need to broaden your cultural horizons. Of course, that's if you're not too busy. I await your reply with a smile.
With Love, Michael

He sat back and opened some mail. It wasn't long before the chime went off on his computer.

My Darling Michael,
You do have a way of making a girl forget everything. I will be free anytime you feel you can whisk me away into a coastal adventure of your liking. Am I getting easy or what? Any special time I can look forward to seeing you?
Lovingly, Tamara

He replied telling her the approximate time he would be at the World Airways Jetport and to dress casual. He called Ernie to get the Falcon 2 ready for the Friday morning flight.

* * * * * * * * * * * * * * * * * * * *

Tamara met him with open arms and even had a Lincoln rented for them. There was one place she had heard about just south of there and he went with her wish to visit it. They parked the Lincoln in the new parking garage across from the Winchester Mansion and walked across the street.

The home was a marvel of architectural workmanship and from the time they stepped into the elevator with their guide, wonders flooded through their eyes. Secret passageways, stairs that let up to nowhere, steps that you went down to get to the next floor higher and the beauty of the woods that were all around them filled their minds. They enjoyed the rifle and gun collection made famous by Winchester. The tour lasted a few hours and they couldn't stop talking about it.

As they were getting ready to leave, the skies had opened up producing a downpour which forced them to put their windbreakers over their heads and run for the car. The weather report on the radio dampened their plans as the entire coast was now under a storm watch, so they decided to head back to the Sheridan. The rains let up around dusk. Not wanting to fight for a parking spot downtown, they took a taxi to one of the comedy palaces and enjoyed the show though some of the dialogue gave a new meaning to the four letter words of the era. A fabulous oriental dinner followed which really made their day end on a high note. Though they arrived back at the Sheridan around nine, it was again, nearing three in the morning before they slipped off to sleep.

Chapter 9

Alameda, California

Decades of time can change many things while only a few things remain constant. Unions of the early years, though once much needed for the common man, had dwindled in numbers. Nationwide crime families, once great in numbers and power, lost both as time and technology took over. They were tolerated in the early years, as not only did they spread fear and death, they also took care of those less fortunate. Bureaucrats put the people on the streets and the crime families fed and protected them. Every major city had these kinds of families and San Francisco was no different. That was then, this was now.

The Bay area families had learned to work together for peace and territory. Occasionally they would lose someone with admirations to rise above the old guard. Frankie Cattalo was one of those men who came west to take a piece of the sacred ground. His partner was Tony Sarino and together they began chipping away small pieces of the three old-line families' in the Bay area. Through gambling, prostitution' and narcotics they began to make a dent in the local families' incomes. The older families' were getting fewer in number each year to where the largest had only nineteen blood members. Cattalo's opposition was going by the way side and took advantage of it. Sarino had ordered several hits on key members and with their flair for magic, someone went to the store and never came back.

Rival street gangs avoided them, as territorial boundaries were honored by Cattalo. The federal agencies, not so much interested in the smaller fry, concentrated their efforts on the big three families. Indictments were very few and far between but just knowing the feds were out there waiting held them in check. A new organizer was sent from the east coast to work with the Vencenti family to open up several new markets. The organizer was an independent operator and was known only to those he had helped in the past. The Vencenti's had never seen him only Cattalo had once. Frankie Cattalo, aware of this information, decided it was a perfect time to substitute one of his people in place of the organizer. He would go inside the local family and shut it down. The organizer was arriving tomorrow night and they would make the exchange in personnel at the organizer's hotel, after he checked in.

Chapter 10

Canon Aero was going through equipment and shop machine upgrading. Michael worked hard with his people to make sure it was done properly and cost effective. Just as he returned from lunch the email flag went up on his computer.

Good Morning Michael,

Thank you so much for the fantastic weekend. I am still a little sore from "walking" on the beach but I'm tough and I'll get through it. In my mind you are still here. I had a physical this morning and I am fit as a fiddle. By the way, what does that saying mean? I have something to talk to you about but I shouldn't in an email, as I know you're very busy. I will say bye for now. I look forward to hearing from you.

All my Love, Tamara

Michael sat back and lit a cigarette. His smile was contagious as thoughts of the weekend flashed through his mind.

Hi Sweetheart,

I could never want for any more than our weekends have given us. As I think back on them, I want to relive them all over again. You are very special to me. Surprisingly, I will be back in the Bay Area in a week for a seminar. Maybe we can drive down the coast to Monterey for a day if you'd like. Remember what you asked me to say to you that morning? I just said it again.

Love, Michael

He had only sat back with his coffee for thirty seconds when Marsha notified him for his next meeting. He went to it with a smile on his face.

Chapter 11

Two Lexus' pulled up in front of the Sheridan and parked in the outside valet aisle. They waited patiently as several taxis came and went.

"You need to make this clean with no witnesses," Cattalo said, as the three put silencers on their automatics. "Make the hit and take him down the stairs to the alley. Legga will be there to take him away."

A few minutes went by when three taxis drove up. Tamara got out of the first one and went inside. An older couple exited the second one and waited for their luggage to be removed. The third taxi contained the man they were waiting for. The man got out and went in. They waited for thirty seconds, then the three got out.

"Oh, Miss Garrett, I think you have something at the front desk," the bellhop said as she waited at the elevator.

She thanked him and headed back to the front desk. The man from the third taxi was just registering when she arrived.

"Hi Larry, I hear you have something for me."

"I'll be right with you Miss Garrett. Let me give this man his key. Here you go, room 1214. Take the second elevator and go straight ahead when you get off."

"Now Miss Garrett, oh yes, you have a package."

She got excited and hoped it was from Michael, just like the flowers he sent every week.

Larry handed her a large envelope which said, The Wharf Shoppe-Photo Enclosed.

She couldn't wait to open it and used the letter opener at the desk. She slid out an eight by ten photo of her and Michael. A big smile broke out on her face.

The three men from the Lexus passed her as she showed Larry the photo.

"Your father is a handsome man. Now I see where you got your good looks," Larry commented as he looked at the picture.

She looked at him then smiled, holding back the laugh that was building. Putting it inside her red coat next to her heart, she half ran half walked to the elevator. She held it tight and couldn't wait to email him about it. The elevator stopped on twelve and the door opened.

The first thing her eyes saw as she stepped off was a man lying on the floor and another man covering him with a plastic tarp. The other two men with guns turned and looked straight at her as she stopped. She reached back for the elevator doors which were now closing. It was as if everything was in slow motion as she stuck her hand into the quickly closing opening which caused the doors to reopen. She slapped the large square button for the lobby then the one labeled Close Door. The doors closed before the two approaching men could get in.

"She saw us Tony, what do we do?" Sal said as he frantically pushed the elevator button.

"This," Sarino said as he fired eight rounds across the elevator door. "Get him out of here."

The elevator to his right opened just then. Sarino got on and pushed the button for the lobby. As he got to the lobby he could hear loud shouting voices, which got louder when the doors opened. A crowd had formed. He went in amongst them to see what they were looking at. "She's dead," he heard several times as he looked down inside the elevator. Tamara was lying face down. Bloodstreams, darker than her red leather coat ran in several directions away from the crimson pool that she lay in. Sarino rose up and straightened his tie. He smiled, then pushed several people out of the way as he casually walked out of the hotel.

Chapter 12

Michael was working late when R.C. knocked and came in and sat down.

"You know it's seven and you should be doing something else than killing yourself here. Want me to order a pizza or something?"

"You're right, I've got people to do this and…"

Michael's phone rang and he hit the speaker.

"Michael Canon, please."

"This is Canon."

"Mr Canon, I'm homicide Detective Sakota with the San Francisco police department. I have a card in my hand to call you in case of emergency."

"What's happened, tell me," Michael said raising his voice.

"A Ms. Tamara Garrett was involved in a shooting at the hotel she was staying at. She was taken to the emergency room. Preliminary reports show she's not expected to pull through."

R.C. stood up and came around next to him. As they listened Michael lost all his strength and sat down in his chair.

"We will be there inside two hours," R.C. said, then hit the button.

Michael was sitting with his head in his hands. R.C. quickly went into the bathroom, wet a towel and returned. It took another minute for Michael to get control of himself.

"Call Ernie then get Kennedy and Mason. Arm them."

"Right, I'll get C.J. too so…"

"No, Goddamn it, get only who I told you. Tell C.J. nothing."

"It's done. Sorry about that Michael."

Michael unlocked his desk drawer, got some cash and his 9mm then walked downstairs. The three met him at his car.

"R.C., I'm sorry for yelling. I need you here to get a team ready if we need to move," Michael said then hugged him.

"I understand, call me," R.C. said as Kennedy drove off.

* * * * * * * * * * * * * * * * * * * *

The Challenger 6 touched down at the World Airways Jetport and a limousine was waiting thanks to R.C. They went straight to the hospital. Mason made inquires and they headed to the sixth floor.

Two patrol officers and a plain clothed man was standing at the end of the hall.

"I'm Michael Canon and you are?"

"Detective Sakota, thanks for coming so quickly. They still have her in surgery."

"Who did this, talk to me."

"First let me ask you do you have permits for those weapons?"

"What? For Christ's sake yes, we do."

"Mr. Canon, I understand you're being somewhat upset and this is understandable but please try to work with us and this will go a lot smoother."

Michael turned from the operating room window, took a breath and let it out.

"Detective Sakota, I do thank you for calling me, but I feel a little anxiety when I'm told my fiancée has just been shot in an elevator of one of the finest hotels in the city. I apologize for being a little hasty to find out what has happened. How was that, better?"

"OK, I didn't mean to imply anything. I can only tell you what I told you and your man on the phone. There were no witnesses to the shooting and I haven't received any word from anyone here at the hospital on her condition."

"Has there been any arrangements to have a guard put at her door?"

"Is there a reason?"

Michael looked at Kennedy then back at Sakota. "No, just thought I'd ask. If you don't mind I will arrange for one of my men to be here at all times, if that is all right with you," Michael said as he tried to keep his voice calm.

"I have no problem with that. If you're going to be here then I will be back in the morning."

"Thank you," Michael said, then turned back to the window.

"I'll stay the first watch Boss," Mason said.

Michael and Kennedy asked for the floor nurse. She told him Tamara was in critical condition with three gunshot wounds. There were two emergency room doctors working on her and she felt it might be several hours more before she would know anything. He thanked her and explained Mason's presence. She understood and arranged to have coffee and a sandwich brought up to him.

"Something is so wrong here," Michael said. "Mason, protect her as you would me. We will be back soon. Call me if something breaks."

"I'll protect her with my life Boss. Nobody will get near her."

They left and headed to the Sheridan.

There were still a lot of people in the hotel lobby when they arrived.

"I would like the key to room 1212," Michael commanded.

"Oh Mr. Garrett, I'm Larry. I recognized you from your picture. I am so sorry about your daughter."

Michael paused for a moment at his statement. "May I have her key Larry?"

"Oh yes sir. I'm here if you need me."

"Thank you."

A folding petition was around the second elevator. Through the opening they could see two workers cleaning up the reddish floor. They took the next elevator to the twelfth floor and got out. They stared at the roped off closed doors with the eight bullet holes in it but said nothing. They walked to Tamara's door and stopped. They looked to the right and saw reddish stains on the floor in front of 1214. They knelt down for a better look at the stains on the light colored carpet.

"Something happened here Boss," Kennedy said as he looked at his red fingertips from touching the stains. "This blood isn't very old."

They went into Tamara's apartment for just a moment then came back out. They stood outside her door and scanned the area with their eyes.

"She got off the elevator, saw a murder or something then must have been seen by whoever did it. She got back on and the killer shot rounds into the elevator. He had to have made sure they had got her so…"

"So, he went down to the lobby to see," Kennedy said, finishing Michael's sentence.

They took the elevator back down and stopped by to see Larry.

"Larry, who was staying in room 1214?" Michael asked.

"I don't think I'm allowed to say anything Mr. Garrett. I mean I could get into…"

Larry stopped talking as Michael put a folded fifty dollar bill on the desk and slid it towards him. Larry put his hand on the bill. "I'll check for you."

"They have video cameras all over the lobby Boss. I wonder if they're being viewed by anyone," Kennedy said as they waited for Larry.

"Here you go Mr. Garrett, the newspaper you asked for," Larry said. "The sports section is good today."

"One other thing Larry, were you were here when this happened?"

"Yes sir, I had just come on. I gave your daughter the envelope that came. Sir, I am really sorry about…"

"Larry, did the police take any of the video tapes that were used in these cameras when they left?"

"Oh wow Mr. Garrett that's a tough one. No, I don't think any of them were removed. Wait a minute, what am I saying, no they didn't because I have the key to the video rooms."

"What do they do with the tapes when they're full, do they store them?"

"Oh no, this is an old hotel. We haven't been updated with computers back there yet. They just use the same ones over, why?"

"Just asking. What time do you go on your break?" Michael asked.

"Actually in a few minutes."

"How about joining us in the coffee shop?"

"Thank you, Mr. Garrett. I could do that. See you there."

They walked into the shop and got a booth. Larry joined them and had some pie and a Coke. Michael asked him about the cameras again and Larry said camera three would be the one facing all of the elevators. Michael asked him about spare tapes in case one of them broke.

"Why didn't you say so, you want to tape a pay movie. I do it all the time. I'll just give you a new clear tape and don't think anything of it."

Michael looked at Kennedy. "Actually, what are the chances Mr. Kennedy here can go with you and pick one out?"

"Well, when I get off break I will be the only one here for an hour so I guess it's all right."

Michael paid the check and they waited as Larry relieved the other man. Larry slipped Kennedy the keys as Michael gave Larry another fifty dollar bill. He was more than thrilled with the money as tips were hard to come by these days. When Kennedy came out they said they would be back soon and then left.

As they drove away Kennedy turned on the local radio station. After one song had played the news came on. They listened as the newscaster told of the shooting at the hotel. They looked at each other when he said the shooting victim was still in surgery and named the hospital. Michael called Mason and told him what they heard and to keep a sharp eye out. They would be right there.

As they approached Mason, one of the doctors came out of the emergency room asking who the relative was. Michael introduced himself and stated he was her fiancé.

"I'm Doctor Wallace, maybe we want to talk in my office."

Kennedy stayed with Mason as Michael accompanied the doctor down the hall where he poured him some coffee then went to his office.

"I hate formalities, please call me Jon. Can I call you Michael?"

"Yes, thank you."

"Your fiancée is very lucky to be alive. She must have nine lives. We removed three 9mm bullets from her. One was lodged near her spine, the second was in her left side, and the third was in her thigh. She may not make it through the night. From the looks of her body she has been in worse situations than this. How did she get those scars, if I may ask?"

"Tamara was a Marine weapons and knife instructor for a number of years."

"Michael, those scars can't be more than a few months old. Please don't misguide me here."

Michael took a deep breath then told the doctor the short version of how she got the wounds and why she was here in San Francisco. He told him to call Agent Sommers or Detective Erickson to verify his story if he needed to.

"I have to hand it to her. She is one incredible young woman."

Michael also told him what he suspected happened to her and how the police were not looking at it his way. The doctor couldn't believe Michael was asking to have her listed as not surviving surgery. When Michael said they might make another attempt on her life here in the hospital, Jon reconsidered.

"It will take some doing but I will list it and make the media aware immediately. If what you say is true many people up here could get hurt."

They left his office and the doctor talked to his staff. Michael watched as they wheeled Tamara into a monitor-filled room and set everything up. He told the team everything he and the doctor discussed. He pulled the newspaper from his pocket that Larry had given him, and opened the sports page. Michael viewed the information on the man in 1214. He told Mason to have a search done on the name even if he had to go through Erickson in Seattle. They needed to look at the tape to see who might have come out of the elevator after the shooting. They needed another copy made also. Kennedy and Mason left. Doctor Wallace gave permission for him to stay the night in her room.

Michael sat down next to her as the monitors and breathing apparatus filled the room with noises one couldn't imagine. He kissed her arm then put his hand on hers. There was no life in her limbs and he felt so helpless. As he looked at her, his emotions took over.

* * * * * * * * * * * * * * * * * * * *

Mason and Kennedy stood at the empty information desk in the hospital lobby and made their calls to R.C. and to Erickson in Seattle. Their network for finding out information was like a pyramid as it started with them and spread out quickly in multi-directions with each person they called. Soon they left for the airport to use the on-board fax machine and computer. As they drove out of the parking lot a Lexus pulled in.

"I'll handle this when we get in. You just make sure I have the time alone with her," Sarino said as he pulled some liquid into a syringe from a small bottle. He put a small rubber cap over the end of the needle then put it in his inside pocket. "Listen," Sal said as a news bulletin came on the radio.

"To follow up on our top story of the day, the woman found shot at the Sheridan earlier this afternoon has died. A hospital official reported she never survived surgery from gunshot wounds inflicted. The authorities are not releasing her identity pending notification of next of kin. In other news..."

"We lucked out this time Tony. That was too close," Sal said as he started the car.

Chapter 13

Michael never left Tamara's side the entire night which had the night nurses in awe of him. They would stop by routinely to check her condition, monitor the readouts, and bring him coffee or anything they could. The doctor walked by at six and Michael went out into the hall.

"We're going to do some more x-rays and scans on her. Why don't you take some time to get something to eat and maybe some rest. I'll let your people know if there's any change," Doctor Wallace said as he looked at her chart.

Michael saw Mason and Kennedy coming up the hallway with Stacy and Arron. Handshakes and hugs went around.

"Thank you all for coming down," Michael said.

"I'll take the first shift with her," Stacy said. "You must be exhausted."

"I can sleep later. Right now we need to find out things. Call me if there's any change."

Michael and the team left to get something to eat. In an hour they drove to the Challenger 6. Michael called Erickson and asked him if he had found out anything but the answer was negative. Mason and Kennedy left to see what they could find out on their own. Michael stretched out on the plane's rear seats and closed his eyes. Molly covered him with a blanket and turned off the rear cabin lights. Arron and Ernie stood guard as they played some cards.

Chapter 14

FBI headquarters
Federal Building
Room 605
Los Angeles, California

"Thank you all for coming today. We would like to welcome those of you from our Seattle and Portland branches of the ATF and DEA," Deputy Director Olin Scarsdale began. "I think congratulations are in order for Special Agent Clayton Sommers and Agent Gerald Kohl for a job well done in Salt Lake. I understand since that time, activity in your areas have de-escalated substantially. We're glad to have you with us."

They received a round of applause from those attending.

"If you haven't read the reports on Salt Lake you need to as this gives us all a better understanding of patterns forming around our region."

They spent the better part of the morning on each separate area of the eleven western states except California. All of the reports showed a decline in many of the crime related areas.

"This brings us to our own state, gentlemen. As you know, we have enjoyed, if that's what we want to call it, peace in the Bay Area for over a year now. In order to nail the lid on the Vencenti crime family we have been working with the Chicago office. They had an operation in place to put an agent on the inside of the family. As you can see from the reports in front of you a red flag has been issued. We haven't heard from our agent in the past twelve hours, since the time he would have checked into the Sheridan hotel. We will continue to monitor this situation. Ok, if there are no questions let's break for lunch and I'll see you at one."

Sommers read the entire report then laid it down. He remembered hearing something about one of the Sheridan hotels but he couldn't recall it. He punched in the hotel's website on the computer. He found the story headlines and hit Print. An agent came up and reminded him it was lunchtime. He folded the printout and put it in his pocket.

Director Scarsdale had already begun talking when Sommers remembered the printout. He read the name of the victim in the shooting, "And she was the fiancée of Michael…"

"Oh shit," Sommers said to himself but not quiet enough for those around him not to hear.

"Agent Sommers, was that a lively comment on what I was saying?"

"Oh no sir, I was just following up on what we were talking about before lunch and I apologize for the choice of words that came out."

"If I recall we were talking about crime families in the Bay Area. Do you have something to add that we might have overlooked?"

"Well not at this moment. A year ago I was on an investigative team sent to monitor the activities on one of the families in San Francisco. If I might request, I would like clearance to be temporarily assigned to your task force there. I know several of the agents in charge and I may be of some help."

"I have you listed to San Diego but I think this can be arranged. Now, let's continue."

Chapter 15

"I wonder if she can she hear me?" Michael asked himself as he sat next to Tamara lightly rubbing her hand and arm. It was killing him to watch her in this state. As the hours went by he brushed her hair and kissed every inch of her face. He had been in the Bay Area twenty-four hours now and he was no closer to finding out who did this to her and why. The Sheridan hotel scenario he discussed with Kennedy was the only way it could have gone down. He was sure of it. He looked up and saw Arron talking to someone who had just walked up. He patted Tamara's hand and then went out into the hall.

"Clay Sommers, good to see you," Michael said as he shook his hand.

"Michael I'm so sorry for what's happened. Is there anything I can do to help?"

"Thank you for asking but for now we can only wait and see. I have been meaning to call you. Do you have some time for me?"

"Of course, how about some breakfast?"

Before they went to eat Michael took Clayton over to the hotel and ran his scenario of the shooting by him. Clay was impressed by his quick assessment of the situation but wasn't surprised. They headed out to get some breakfast.

"Michael we need to let the authorities handle this investigation. They're a fine department and I'm sure something will turn up very soon," Sommers said as Stacy handed him some creamers for his coffee. The four ordered their food.

"I was crushed to hear Tamara was killed and am so thankful she is alive. My biggest shock came when your name was mentioned in the paper. All I could think was world war two was going to start again. Michael, if you find out who did this before the authorities do, you have to promise me you will let them handle it. What do you say?"

"Clay, I have talked to the police and even had John Erickson make some inquiries. They have nothing. There is something I would like you to do for me."

"Sure, anything."

Michael held his hand out and Kennedy put the hotel tape in it.

"Tell me who the man is that comes out of the elevator then leaves."

"How the hell did you come by this? Goddamn it Michael, this is tampering with evidence in an investigation."

"The police made their quote-unquote investigation then left the scene for the night. We acquired this five minutes before it was to be recycled. The local investigators didn't even consider this. Now, are you going to find out for me what I want to know or not?"

Sommers just sat with his eyes closed as the server placed their orders in front of them.

"You know by me having this you've made me an accessory after the fact. You can't keep doing this."

"Why can't you help us Mr. Sommers? We're only trying to find out the truth. Is that so wrong?" Stacy asked.

"Oh Stacy, it's not that. It's the method in which Michael goes about things. There are rules we go by and everything has to fit. Ok, yes, I will run it through our computers and see what I can find out. Until then you will have to step down. Give me a few days?"

"I will give you until seven this evening. That's twelve hours then I will put my people on it," Michael answered.

"Hold on a minute Canon, you can't threaten the authorities let alone a federal officer…"

"It's Canon now is it? Let me put it another way. The doctors said they would know in twelve hours if Tamara will live. I've given you the same time frame. I will stay out of it for that same period of time, but hear me well, Special Agent Clayton Sommers, if she dies then there will be a funeral. We will leave right afterwards. As a friend you can't be here when we come back."

Sommers ran his tongue across his lips that were now all of a sudden dry. He looked at Stacy, then Kennedy, and then Michael. Their steel piercing looks went right through him. He knew first hand what Michael and his team could do, so he made his choice.

"Thank you Michael, for giving me until seven," he answered, then picked up his coffee with a somewhat shaky hand.

Sommers left and the three went back to the airport to the others. Michael had laid down the gantlet and now would wait.

Chapter 16

Frank Cattalo had completed his plan and his man was now in place inside the Vencenti family walls. He would wait to find the weakness and the strengths of his nemesis on the hill and then take him down. He was recruiting his shooters and lieutenants from the outside and two men had arrived today from New Orleans. By the week's end he would have over a dozen more.

* * * * * * * * * * * * * * * * * * * *

Sommers called in several favors from agents he knew at the San Francisco bureau. They arranged for Sommers to join in on a high-level meeting called for eleven that morning.

"Gentlemen, we have an unanticipated problem I must bring you up to date on," Special Agent Brian Centers began. "We have been working with several other agencies to close down all operations within one of the crime families. On a sting operation initiated two weeks ago we intercepted and took into custody one Raymond David Garzi, aka the organizer. For immunity from prosecution he laid out his plans for coming to the Bay area. We were able to substitute one of our agents that had been following the Vencenti family for years. Monday night he had a meeting set up with Vencenti to begin working for him from within their organization. After he left the airport he checked into the Sheridan. Bloodstains found outside his room have come back matching his DNA. We are ruling out Vencenti, as he had only to gain by his presence. We must now concentrate on the other two families. Any questions?"

"Who else would stand to gain from this? How about some of the smaller street bosses?"

"Good question, Agent Sommers. We don't feel the smaller bosses have the power to force an all out war between the families. First of all they wouldn't even consider a war like those in the past. No, I see no reason to move in that direction."

The meeting ended soon and nothing more than information of the obvious went around. As Clay left the briefing room one of the agents handed him a large manila envelope. He sat down at a vacant desk and opened it. He read the printout and looked at a mug shot taken by the Denver police in 1985. He slipped everything back in with the surveillance tape.

"Steven, does the name Anthony Sarino ring any bells to you?" Sommers asked one of the agents near him.

"Yeah, he's pretty low profile. I think he used to hang with a Frank Catano, or Cattalo, or someone like that. Why are you asking?"

"Oh nothing, just running names through my head."

He went to the computer and punched up the names he was given and waited for the printout.

Chapter 17

It was killing Michael to wait even though he had nothing to work on. He walked off the Challenger 6 and headed slowly towards a row of small planes to his right.

"Can I walk with you Boss?" he heard Stacy say.

"Sure, what's on your mind Speedy?" he said putting his arm around her shoulders.

"Are we going to get the team together again? I mean is it looking like we might go up against someone?"

"I don't know Stacy; we don't have enough to go on right now."

"Did you mean what you said to Agent Sommers this morning?"

"You know I'm all talk and no bite," Michael said as he squeezed her. "Guys like Sommers and Erickson live by the rules. You have to put the fear of God into them to get them to do anything."

"I knew that, that's why I love ya."

"Well, I love you too, so there."

She put her hand on his at her shoulder. "You know Tamara loves you also."

"I know that, I love her too."

Stacy stopped and came in front of him. "No, I mean she really does love you. This is so wonderful what you're doing for her."

Michael put his hands on her shoulders. "Listen Speedy, I really do love her for real."

She gave him a big hug then a short kiss. He smiled as they turned around and they walked back to the Challenger 6.

Molly prepared him and several others a sandwich. They talked about a worse case scenario and then Michael left for the hospital.

* *

The doctor was leaving Tamara's room when he arrived.

"Most of her signs are positive. This is the time she should be coming around but we're getting little response. We're monitoring her closely."

Michael thanked him and went in next to her. She laid there pretty much tube free now except for the small oxygen piece at her nose. Her arms were black and blue where all the needles were inserted. He kissed the tip of her nose and lips then sat down. The nurse left and he started talking to her in a soft low tone. Soon he laid his head on her arm and felt her warmth. In a few minutes he thought he felt a slight movement in her fingers as he moved his hand slightly. He laid his head back down on her shoulder and watched her hand. He squeezed it about every ten seconds. On the last squeeze she moved her little finger against his. He sat up then looked at her. Her lips moved ever so slightly. He looked out in the hall but no nurses were in sight. He kissed her on the lips several times very softly. She moved them again and swallowed. He felt several fingers move and looked down at her hand.

"You forgot my…eyes."

His head turned back quickly. She was looking at him and she tried to smile slightly. Michael's eyes began to tear as he put his head next to hers. "Is that all you ever think about, romance?"

"Yes," he heard softly from her.

The nurse and doctor came in. Wallace asked for a few minutes with her. Michael wiped his eyes as he went out. Five minutes later Doctor Wallace came out.

"She is healing very nicely but there are several things we still have to check. It will be a few more hours before you can see her again so I'll give you five minutes with her now."

"What's wrong?"

"I'll have more answers when you get back."

Michael held her gently. She asked him if she was going to be all right. He tried to assure her she would.

"Hey, would you have gone and let me kiss your lips all night without opening your eyes?"

She smiled. "Yes, I was enjoying that but you forgot to kiss my eyes like you do."

"Well, I'll have a lot of time to do that when you're out of here."

"Do you really mean that? Can we go someplace?"

"I sure do, where would you like to go?"

"The Bahamas. I always wanted to go there and swim nude in the warm water."

"It's as good as done. Keep that thought with you until I get back."

He walked out slowly still watching her smile.

* * * * * * * * * * * * * * * * * * * *

Stacy came over to pick him up and felt relieved Tamara was awake and talking. Sommers called and wanted to meet. Michael told him they were heading to the plane.

Sommers laid out what he found and asked what was next. Michael placed his file on top of the printouts.

"I think we know pretty much the same," Michael said. "Our source also had these names as associates of Cattalo."

Sommers wrote down the names in his notepad. "I'm not going to ask where you got these names."

"Good," Michael answered as he looked at his watch.

"Michael, I got you what you asked for, now what are you going to do?"

"I want to know everything about these people. I don't care how you get it. I won't do anything without telling you first. How's that?"

"I can live with that," Sommers said as he got up and walked out with Michael.

"I won't wait too long Clay, I need answers. I also need an informant who knows them. If I work this right, you and your colleagues will get the media headlines. As far as we're concerned, all of this never happened."

Michael went back at the hospital and met up with Doctor Wallace. They went to his office.

"How's she doing?"

"Michael I have to say I'm very impressed with her recuperative powers. Her external wounds are stable. There are two things that we need to talk about, that's why I brought you in here."

"She is going to recover isn't she?" Michael asked.

"Yes she will."

"Then what?"

"I am sorry about losing the baby. She was only in her first trimester. Maybe if she hadn't lost so much blood we might have saved the fetus. There is a possibility she may never be able to bear children."

Michael sat there in total wonderment.

"She has other complications. The major problem we have is she's lost the ability of movement and sensation in the entire lower part of her body. We believe the bullet we removed from her spine area caused considerable damage to the nerve fibers located around it."

"You're saying she's paralyzed from the waist down?" Michael asked.

"We did another workup on her after you left. She does have intensive swelling in the spine area. In the time she has been immobile that swelling should have decreased by half. I can't say that it won't, but unless it dissipates by fifty percent in the next twenty-four hours, she may never walk again."

Michael put his fingers to his now closed eyes. Thoughts of her flashed through his mind like if he was remembering someone from the past. He opened his eyes. "How good is your neurosurgeon?"

"He's one of the best."

"I'm not sure how to ask this but is it possible to bring in another without damaging the trust in your surgeon?"

"Doctor Blake and I have already talked about it and have the hospital's permission to go outside. Doctor Jason Ambler at the Mayo Clinic in Minnesota is the top man in the field. I took the liberty and called him. He said he would come. The problem is the airline worker's strike and getting him here by tomorrow is not good."

Michael told him to hold on a moment. He called Ernie at the plane and asked him about the trip and if he could refuel even though there was a workers strike going on. He told Ernie to hold on.

"Can he be ready and waiting in five hours?" Michael asked.

"Yes."

"Ernie, fuel up. Your destination is Rochester, Minnesota. One of you will fly the plane up and the other will bring it back."

As Michael gave him the person to pick up, Wallace called Blake and told him what they were doing. He said he would be waiting. A nurse bought them in some coffee.

"Michael, I don't know what to say. This is going to be very expensive for you."

"Shouldn't we be sending x-rays and charts or something along for him to look at?"

"He already has them on his computer."

"Does she know?"

"No, it's better we wait."

"Can I see her?"

"By all means and Michael, thank you again."

Michael told himself he had to put anything negative out of his mind as he walked past the nurse's station. He stopped and backed up next to a vase of flowers. He asked if he could have one and they said yes. He entered her room to a face that barely broke a smile. He came around the bed and gave her the carnation. She held her right arm up and he bent down to her. She began crying as she held him as tight as she could, which wasn't much. He slowly sat down without breaking her light hold.

"Michael, I have no feeling in my legs or feet. I'm so scared."

"I know, I have already spoken with the doctor."

She let him up and he gave her his handkerchief.

"If you blow your nose on that then you have to wash it," he said with a smile.

She wiped her eyes and smiled. She picked up the flower and smelled it. Color was coming back into her face.

"What's happening Michael, can you tell me?"

"Ever smash you toe and it swelled up really big and hurt like hell?"

"Yes, once when I was a teenager. It hurt for a week."

"The hurt was caused by pressure pushing out. Right now everything is healing up fine except your back where there is pressure built up against the spine itself. The doctors can do two things. First they can wait until it goes down by itself, kinda like your toe did, or they can go in and try to relieve it."

"Will that bring back all the feeling?"

"That's what we're hoping for. Since they are trying to get rid of you because they need the bed for someone who really is sick, I'm going for option number two."

She smiled at his way of putting serious things in a humorous way.

"I want to do what you think is best. Who's going to do the surgery? Is he good?"

"The best in the country is in the upper mid-west. I've sent Ernie to pick him up. He'll be here before the sun wakes up."

"What am I going to do with you?" she asked.

"You mean right here, right now, in the hospital?"

He leaned over and kissed her as she pinched him as hard as she could.

"What happens if they can't relieve the pressure; and be honest with me?"

"Then we'll get married, live in a cabin by a big lake and I'll take care of you the rest of our lives."

They both had glassy eyes as he bent down and held her.

Doctor Wallace started to come in but backed away as he knew she was getting the best therapy there was.

"I'm getting so tired my darling, why don't you go get some coffee and I'll see you in a little while."

"Close your eyes and think of us nude in the Bahamas," he said as he kissed her.

Losing his family to the Canarra was tougher than what he had just endured. He was ripped apart inside but it was nothing to what he knew she must have been going through. Stacy and Kennedy found him sitting on a chair just outside her room. Wallace came by and told them the sedative he had given her had finally kicked in so she would sleep all night.

"I've got the watch, Michael. Stacy will take you back to the motel."

They walked out and headed away from the hospital. Stacy asked about Tamara's condition and he told her everything up to now but not the worse case scenario.

"R.C. said to tell you everything was going well at Aero and to not worry about anything but getting this taken care of. He had one of the Escalades flown down so you would have something safe around you."

"That R.C. is something. I hated to see him get the short end of the picnic we had but he lives for those days. I think we all needed that to bring us back down."

"That was the most fun I'd had in years. I love our team."

"I feel bad about the guys doing double duty. Kennedy looked exhausted. He's always here to relieve me," Michael commented.

Stacy laughed. "He's been smitten by one of the ten to six shift nurses. She brings him food and drinks all night long."

"Kennedy, no way. Really?"

"Oh yeah, and he's got it bad. They were at her place for the past four hours. I think it's beautiful."

"He rarely has matching socks on. My God, what am I doing to the team?"

They had purchased a block of rooms at the Southern Inn just off the airport and Michael took one. His body was ready to give out but his mind was still at its high peak. He prayed tomorrow would bring the news about Tamara he hoped for.

Chapter 18

Stacy woke Michael at five with coffee telling him the Challenger was less than an hour out. He got dressed and they left for the airport. Soon after they got there they watched the plane touch down and taxi to their location.

Stacy brought the Lincoln up. Mason took the passenger seat and they left. Michael called Doctor Wallace and said they were on their way.

"I want to thank you for coming Doctor Ambler. I hope your flight wasn't too cramped," Michael said.

"Best flight I ever had, and what a nice plane. I may never fly on one of those big ones again."

Stacy pulled up in front of the hospital and they were met by Wallace, the hospital chief of staff and two others. They greeted Ambler warmly. The party went to the chief of staff's office and Michael went to see Tamara. The nurses gave him another flower without him even asking.

"Hi bright eyes, how's my girl?"

They kissed and she accepted the flower. Michael motioned to Stacy to come in. Tamara couldn't have been happier for the few minutes she stayed. Michael gave them both a couple of tissues from the box. He watched his two girls and the bond they shared together as friends. Stacy said she would see her soon then left.

"So I'm your girl, don't I have something to say about that?"

"Well, yes I think you should. What do ya say?"

She thought for a long moment and tried to fight back a laugh.

"Ok, I kinda like the sound of you're my guy."

He told her about Ambler arriving and there was nothing to be worried about. "Did you fall asleep last night dreaming about the Bahamas?"

"You know I did. I can't wait to do it for real."

The door opened and both doctors came in.

"Hi Tamara, I'm Doctor Ambler. Hey, I like the color in your cheeks. That's a good sign."

"Hi Doctor. Michael was just telling me about you getting here."

"He's a fine man that Michael and he said if we make you well he will give me another ride in his plane. How's that for an incentive," he said smiling.

"I have confidence in you."

"You'll be out of here before you know it. I will be back a little later."

Michael thanked the doctors as they left.

"I like him. I know he will do what he says," Tamara said as Michael sat on the edge of the bed.

They talked for nearly an hour about their trip to the Wharf. He told her about the vacation packages to the Caribbean he found on the internet. He told her of Kennedy's new romance and she got tickled. Her spirits couldn't have been higher as the nurses arrived to get her prepared for her next ordeal. Wallace told him it would be several hours before they would know anything.

As they drove back Stacy said she thought they were being followed. Michael and Mason pulled their 9mm's and cocked them. They watched a light green Ford move up on them from behind. Blue lights began to flash in the car's grill for about six seconds then they went off. Stacy pulled over then laid her automatic next to her. It was Sommers. He got out of the Ford and into the backseat.

"I have good news and not so good news," Sommers began. "Here is the name of one of their informers who knows Cattalo."

"And the bad news," Michael asked.

"There are no new leads in the case."

"This is not helping my confidence level," Michael said. "Where do we find mister wonderful here?"

"He cleans up a tattoo parlor just south of the Embarcadero. He always wears blue jeans and red sneakers. The address is on the back. Remember he works for us. Oh, here are Tamara's things from that night. I thought you'd like to have them," he said handing Michael a large envelope.

Michael thanked Sommers as he left then they drove back to the motel.

He cleaned up and changed his shirt. He opened the envelope Sommers had given him with Tamara's things in it. He smiled as he looked at matchbooks and napkins she had saved from the restaurant the night she got her new coat. He slid out the photo of the two of them which was inside a sealed plastic cover. A third of the front and most of the back showed reddish brown dried bloodstains. There was a bullet hole right in the middle of it. He looked at it then kissed her face through the plastic. He called the team together for a meeting in Kennedy's room.

"Shawn, what are you doing?" Mason asked.

"R.C. sent all our gear down so I was seeing if our bionic arms would stick out with our sport coats on. I don't think we'll have a problem. Besides, I kinda miss the feel of the Kevlar shirts underneath," Kennedy answered.

Michael and Stacy agreed they weren't noticeable. Mason put his on also. They decided to pay the informant a visit and see what they could find out. They left for the Embarcadero area of town.

* *

They located the shop and parked across the street from it. They watched as mostly men went in and out.

"There he is, jeans and red shoes," Stacy said as they all looked to the left.

Stacy remained in the Escalade as the three crossed the street.

Loud rock music blared as they entered the shop. It looked like an old converted barbershop with three chairs up front then partitions along both walls. They got a good look-over from four guys up front as they walked to the center of the shop. Michael asked who was in charge.

"What do ya want?" the first guy on the right said.

"I'm looking for Johnnie Lima," Michael said as he looked around.

"Never heard of him, try somewhere else."

Michael asked him again and got the same response. The radio on the shelf next to Mason was blaring which made it hard to hear. Michael looked at Mason and nodded his head towards the radio. Mason raised his arm and sent the radio and shelf crashing down to the floor. The tattooed guy dropped his needle gun and stood up.

"Hey…what the hell are you doing?"

"Where's Johnnie Lima? I won't ask again."

The guy looked around then towards the back of the shop. He smiled and said, "Why didn't you say so in the first place. Hey John-boy, come on out."

Two tattoo-laden guys in undershirts appeared between the partitions. They would have fitted in better at one of the muscle building gyms lifting five hundred pound barbells, but they were here now and they didn't look particularly happy. The four they passed coming in started to approach but stopped when Michael pointed his 9mm at them. Mason and Kennedy moved just in front of Michael.

The two musclemen lunged at them. Kennedy extended his arms catching his man at the shoulders which stopped him cold. Kennedy raised him off the ground as if he weighed nothing and threw him into the partition on the left. Mason's man came in headfirst and Brock brought his knee up quickly and caught him in the forehead which brought his entire body up. Brock hit him across the face, left to right with his titanium forearm sending him headlong into the man with the mouth's desk and beyond. With the left partition flattened from Kennedy's man, Michael could see their man cowering down. Michael looked at the tattooed guy and said, "Well?"

"Hey Lima, get out here, now."

A man in his early thirties appeared very cautiously and came within several feet of Michael.

"Word has it you borrowed one of my trucks over the weekend and now the police have it. Talk to me," Michael said as Kennedy moved behind him.

"Hey, I don't know what you're talking about. I wasn't even there, I swear," the kid said looking at the shop owner.

"Bring em," Michael said, then turned and walk towards the front door.

The four guys between them and the door moved back against the wall as Michael cocked his automatic.

"Hey, what about my shop. Who's gonna pay for this?"

Mason stopped next to the last barber chair and looked back at the guy. He grabbed the chair and twisted it once which ripped the lag bolts out of the floor. He then picked it up and sent it through the closest partition. It came to rest against another chair.

Michael stopped and looked back at the guy then the three left.

Stacy quickly brought the Escalade just past the front of the shop and they all got in. She drove away quickly. Lima sat between Mason and Kennedy and had no idea what was next.

"Relax Johnnie, Sommers asked us to pay you a visit," Michael said, as he handed the guy a cigarette.

He took one in his shaking hand. Mason lit it for him.

"What does he want, I mean, you want?"

"We understand you know a Tony Sarino. Talk to me."

"Hey man, I don't know what…"

His denial ended when Kennedy began to squeeze his forearm.

"Ok…Ok. I know of him."

"I want to know where he's at, what he does, and who's with him. Write it down, all of it," Michael said, handing him a pad and pen.

Mason rolled down the window, grabbed his cigarette and threw it out. Lima began to write like crazy. He handed it back to Michael who looked over the chicken scratches.

"This is it? How do you call him?"

Kennedy gripped down on his forearm again.

"Oh yeah, I forgot."

Lima told them the number then asked what they were going to do with him.

"It's for sure you can't go back looking the way you do," Michael stated. "Stacy, slow to twenty-five."

"We may need to talk to you again so be handy," Michael said, then motioned to Mason with his head.

"Hey, you can't do this, I mean Sommers promised..."

Mason slid open the side door and flung the kid out.

They watched as he bounced several times and hit the curb ending up on the grass by the walkway. They saw him get up and stagger around. They headed back to the motel.

"Ya know Boss that was kinda fun. You gotta love these arms," Mason said as he lit a cigarette.

"I think he thought you were going to do him in," Stacy laughed.

"Hey, what did he think that we were the violent types?" Michael said as he lit up.

They all got a good laugh.

Back at the motel Michael cleaned up and then headed to the hospital with Kennedy.

"How are you fixed for money Shawn?" Michael asked.

"Oh I'm stretching what I have."

Michael gave him three hundred and told him to take her out to someplace nice.

"How did you know I was, oh, Stacy. Can't anyone keep a secret anymore?"

"It wasn't Stacy, I just don't miss much. When we get back I'm going to get you some eyeglasses or contacts."

"Why would you do that, I mean I can see fine."

He saw Michael looking down at his feet.

"Oh, I see."

"Are you wearing the arms? I don't want you crushing her when you give her a hug."

He said he wasn't as he rushed off to meet his date.

Michael met with Wallace who informed him surgery went well and Tamara should be coming around soon. It would be tomorrow before they could tell anything more. He went in and sat with her for several hours. It was breaking his heart to see her like this and knew once she was out he would have a lot of making up to do. He looked out into the hallway and saw Shawn talking to a nurse. His smile lit up the hallway so he knew she was the one. She left him for a moment and came into the room.

"Hi, I'm Catherine. I brought you some coffee."

"That was very kind of you," Michael said as he stood up. She was about six feet tall and he knew she was a good match for the six-four Kennedy.

"We're all pulling for her. Oh, you forgot to pick this up on your way by," she said as she reached down in her pocket. She carefully brought out a short stemmed carnation. Michael thanked her as she went back out with Shawn. He put the carnation in Tamara's hand so she would see it when she woke up if he wasn't there.

As he sat next to her, he thought of a plan to draw Sarino out but knew it would be dangerous if they were found out. He thought it might be better to go right to the top with Cattalo to cut out any more intermediaries. He stepped out into the hallway, called R.C. and they discussed it. He looked at Tamara all the time he talked just in case she woke. He told R.C. what they did at the tattoo parlor and R.C. wished he had been there to see it all.

"I can't believe you actually threw the kid out of the truck. The guys here will love that when I tell them."

"Hey, he couldn't go back untouched and I felt having Mason or Kennedy work him over would be too much."

"Oh so you just chucked him from a speeding vehicle. I thought I taught you better than that but I guess not," R.C. said laughing. "Keep me informed, I worry about you down there son."

"Well if I come back there you said you're gonna whip my ass so I'm safer here."

They both laughed as they hung up.

As he reentered her room he saw her hand move as the flower rose up a little. He kissed her lips lightly then kissed her eyes. He sat down and took her hand. Soon she began to come out of the anesthesia. He felt her hand squeeze around his fingers. He put his face up to hers and talked to her. He touched her face and hair then kissed her again. Her lips moved and he knew she was almost there. A minute later he heard, "Where's my coffee?"

He smiled and put his face next to hers. "I remembered to kiss your eyes."

"I know. I felt you."

In a minute she had her eyes opened and he held her. He told her what Wallace told him and not to worry. She kept falling in and out of sleep as the anesthesia was still with her. Several hours later Catherine and a nurse's aide came in. Catherine introduced her as Candice. Michael kissed Tamara as Catherine said they were going to put her to sleep again. Tamara told him she loved him as she closed her eyes.

Chapter 19

Michael headed back to the motel. Sommers was waiting for him and he wasn't in a good mood.

"Have you seen the news on TV? For Christ's sake, I thought you were going to do this quietly?"

"Here it is Boss," Arron said, as he turned the volume up on the set.

"And then this one guy picks up that bolted down barber chair over there and threw it at me like it's a feather. I barely got out of the way."

"Well, whomever they were that stopped by the Tattoo Shop today, police say they have no clues to their identity. This is Sharron Cameron, Channel 11 news"

"I didn't throw that at him but now I wish I had," Mason said as he looked at Sommers.

"Had I known you were going to throw Johnnie Lima out of your car I wouldn't have told you who he was. Damn it Michael."

"Have you gotten any information on Cattalo for me yet?" Michael asked.

"Yes, but now I'm not sure I'm gonna give it to you. What are you gonna do next, throw him out of your plane?"

Michael looked at Mason and said, "Make a note of that, we haven't tried that one."

Sommers threw his hands up and walked back and forth across the room.

"Relax Clay, I have Cattalo's number right here too. I'm going to call him and set up a meeting. Want to join us?"

"No and I don't want to see it on the news tomorrow. How'd you come by the number?"

"From the guy we threw…"

"I know, out of the speeding car."

"Hey, we saved his life. Had he gone back to the Tattoo parlor clean-shaven they would have known something was up. It was either the street or Mason. Which would you have rather had?"

He looked over at Mason. "All right, I see your point. You have all I have on Frankie Cattalo. Be careful though, he acts on impulse."

"So do we Clay, stop worrying. I'll call you when it's over, the meeting that is."

"How is Tamara? Stacy told me you brought somebody in to try and help her. That was nice of you."

"Thank you. She survived the surgery but it's too early to tell on how it went."

They talked a few minutes more then Sommers left.

Stacy opened some coffee she had gotten from the motel lobby and handed it to Michael. The others got comfortable as Michael called Cattalo.

"This is Cattalo, who's this?"

"Right now let's say I'm someone who can help you."

"What kind of help?"

"A mutual friend of yours, who will remain nameless for the time being, has come into San Francisco and damaged some of my goods. I think we need to have a sit-down and discuss this."

"I don't even know you. What makes you think I'm interested in a meeting with you?"

"It's in both of our interests. I might even be able to help you with Vencenti when the time comes."

There was a long silence on the phone.

"Make it a public place and you can bring two of your people with you," Michael said to break the silence.

"Ok, Fisherman's Wharf, Catalina outdoor café in an hour."

"This is a safe sit-down. I respect the code. I know you will also," Michael added.

"It's agreed."

"What code is that Boss?" Kennedy asked when Michael hung up.

"Beats the hell out of me. It was in a movie I rented a month ago. It worked then, let's hope it works here."

They put the address of the meeting place into the laptop computer and printed out a map. They zoomed in and Michael told Arron to take a position not far from there with his sniper rifle in case the meeting was a trap. Stacy would be shopping nearby also. They left and headed to the Wharf.

To Michael's liking there were a lot of people there. He sat down at a table with his back to the ocean. Kennedy and Mason stood behind him leaning back on the railing. They waited for ten minutes then three men approached.

"This is a nice place to have a meeting wouldn't you say?" Michael asked.

"It would. I'm Frank Cattalo. This is Tony and Sal."

"My name is Canon, please," Michael said motioning him to sit.

Cattalo looked at Mason and Kennedy who stood silently.

"Mr. Cattalo, I have heard a lot about you and from that I think we can come to an understanding with a problem I'm having."

"Let's talk Mr. Canon and see where it goes."

"I understand you have an acquaintance or know of a..."

Michael paused for a moment and turned his head to Mason who bent down to his ear then stood back up. Cattalo saw Mason's .45 inside his jacket then looked at Kennedy who was staring at him.

"An Anthony Sarino."

"Sure, I know of him."

"Before we go any further, my men get very troubled when there are people moving around."

Cattalo looked at Sal who had slowly moved around to the right side of Michael.

"Sally, come back over here, behind me."

"Thank you."

"I apologize. They're new people, you know how it is."

"This Mr. Sarino has taken a young woman away from a very important friend of mine. You may have seen it in the papers."

"That thing at the hotel?"

Michael nodded his head slightly.

"That was a terrible tragedy. My condolences to your friend."

"Word on the street tells him it was this Mr. Sarino and we are here to bring him back to my friend, if at all possible."

"What do you want from me Mr. Canon?"

"You are someone moving up, this we know, but you need help in certain areas of your, let's say, endeavor. You bring Mr. Sarino to us in the morning before we fly out and a whole new world could open up before you. The key to a city maybe."

Cattalo sat there for a moment pondering Michael's words.

"If I can't do this, then what?"

Michael just shrugged his shoulders slightly.

"But if I can deliver, how do I contact you?" he asked quickly.

Michael reached over his shoulder and Kennedy handed him a piece of paper, which he handed to Cattalo.

"We will wait until seven o'clock to hear from you. After that we'll be gone."

"You said something about Vencenti on the phone."

"So I did. My friend can give you Vencenti but he must know who will work with him. A personal favor for…a key let's say. Goodbye, Mr. Cattalo."

Cattalo stood up and extended his hand. When he did Mason and Kennedy took a step forward putting their hands inside their coats. Michael held his hand up, and then stood up. He shook his hand firmly.

They watched Cattalo and his men walk away then proceeded to the Lincoln. They met the others at the motel.

"My God Boss, you had me nearly pissing in my pants. What movie did you watch? That was a work of art," Kennedy said as he sat down hard on the bed laughing.

"Hell, it was like a scene right out of a gangster movie," Mason said with a smile. "I was ready to shoot all three of them."

"It went well tonight people. Damn, his hands were sweating and it wasn't even hot out."

They all laughed.

Chapter 20

They were up at four to get ready. Michael called Sommers and told him how it went. Sommers was relieved they didn't kill anybody. Michael chuckled.

At six the cell phone rang. Kennedy wrote down some instructions on a pad then hung up. They were to go south to the empty transit parking lot and park along the back, then Sarino would be delivered. The meeting was in one hour. They all knew it was a trap.

"I'm going alone," Stacy said as she stepped into her Kevlar gear. "If you're going to be near I can hear your every word."

Michael was hesitant at first but let her take the lead.

Mason drove the Lincoln to a location above the transit lot in an old residential area. From there Michael and Kennedy could be in direct contact with Stacy and view the situation.

Stacy drove the Escalade slowly to the location in the lot and stopped. A car faced them from the rear corner of the lot about a hundred feet away. They saw two men get out, walk to the front of the car and stop. Michael's cell phone rang.

"Here he is Mr. Canon, just like you asked. Blink your lights and we'll bring him to you."

Kennedy informed Stacy of the request.

"Thank you, here he comes."

Just then two cars roared up on the left side of them. Its occupants opened up on them with their automatic rifles. Bullets penetrated the outside shell of the Escalade but didn't go through the plate R.C. had installed. The bulletproof glass cracked from the weapon's fire but nothing came through. After about ten seconds the cars sped away including the one in front of them.

It took Mason less than a minute to get to the Escalade. Kennedy slid open the side door to find Stacy a little shaken but all right.

A light green sedan with a flashing red light on the dash came up to them quickly. Sommers got out.

"Did you get all that?" Michael asked.

"I can't believe you went this far. I thought you were all dead for Christ's sake."

"Everybody gone?"

"Yes, they scattered like flies. Now what?"

"On to plan B," Michael said as he shut the side door and Stacy started the engine.

"Plan B? What the hell is plan B?" Sommers yelled as they drove away.

Chapter 21

Special Agent Sommers was still having a problem with Michael playing an independent role in the area. The agency still didn't have enough to take Cattalo down let alone the families who were in totally legitimate businesses. He could never second-guess Michael as Michael did spontaneous and unthinkable things. Figuring him out was next to impossible. Sommers couldn't even take the taped attack on them to his higher ups as it didn't show a crime being initiated. It just showed someone using a truck for target practice which was a misdemeanor at best.

* *

Michael spent several hours at the hospital as Tamara had awakened shortly after he arrived. It meant everything to her to have him at her side. The nurses and aides came in and Michael waited outside the room. The head nurse informed him doctor Wallace needed to see him in his office.

"Michael, we've done all we can do. Our latest tests and scans have shown some improvement to the spinal region. We can't reduce the pressure below fifty percent though. To put it another way, her system isn't helping the problem, it's accepting it. This happens in such cases as these," Wallace explained.

"What else can we do? Hell, you can reattach people's limbs back on, there has to be something," Michael said in desperation.

"I am very sorry about the outcome Michael. We did all we could. In time maybe some procedure will be found to reverse this anomaly but for now we can do no more," Ambler said.

"How about something in its experimental stage, surely someone is working on a problem like this."

"Yes, there is work being done in this area but even if we could do something, her body cannot take anymore now. To put her under again could be fatal. I'm sorry," Doctor Ambler said.

Michael sat there for a moment then asked if she knew. They said no but would tell her later today. Michael said he would, and then stood up.

"Doctor Ambler, I thank you for coming to help us. I will have the plane standing by to take you home. This has meant a lot to both of us to have you come. Thank you again."

Michael handed him a business card and told him to send him a bill for his services. He called Ernie to get ready for a return flight. They shook hands and he left the office.

Michael went to the washroom and threw some water on his face. This wasn't getting any easier for him as he walked to her room. As he entered she had a smile on her face and he created one of his own.

"Hi. Is that my guy coming to see me?"

"None other. What are you up to?"

"Oh, just waiting to see you. I missed you."

"Me too. How would you like for me to get you a portable CD player with good headphones so you can listen to some music?"

"That's a great idea. See, you think of everything."

She wrote down songs she liked.

"Michael, I need to talk to you about something."

"Sure, anything."

"Remember when I told you I had a surprise for you when you came down next time?"

"Yes."

"My doctor told me I was going to have a baby and I couldn't tell you on the phone. I wanted you with me but…"

Michael put his face next to hers as she began to cry.

"I know all about it. It's not the end of the world."

"Yes, it is. Doctor Wallace said I may never have another child because of my injuries."

"I should have used protection but I never thought of it. I guess I thought you were using something."

"Michael, I didn't do it on purpose. I have never used anything. I wanted a child by you so badly. I wasn't going to force you into any marriage if that's what's bothering you."

"Hey, put that thought out of your head right now," Michael said sitting up. "It just happened a little sooner than I expected, that's all."

"It's all over now Michael. I believe things happen for a reason. I'll be out of your life soon and you can go on with yours."

Michael looked at her closed wet eyes. He couldn't believe what he was hearing.

"Do you think I fell in love with you because you could bear children? That is something I figured would happen in time. I was both happy and sad when I heard."

"You don't understand Michael, I am no use to you anymore. I'm scarred, barren, and it looks like I'll never walk again. You don't need that."

"Since it looks like we're having our first argument, who made you the expert on what I need? Let's just see what I have. I have two plants in two different states. I have two aircraft to use as I see fit. I have two doctors taking care of the woman I just happen to love. No, I'm not going to accept your irrational thinking. We're going to get you out of here and we, that is you and I as in two people, are going to do things together. You think about that."

Tamara raised her arms up and Michael leaned into them. She pulled him next to her and held him. "I'll try."

He put off telling her the outcome of the surgery by saying they still wanted to let the pressure work its way out. She kind of sensed he was holding something back. The nurses needed to come in. He told her he had to go back to the plant in Reno but would be back in the morning.

* *

When he arrived at the motel he was in for a surprise. Four of the Seattle five were waiting for him.

"Hey Jim you're looking well. Brian, Chad, Paul. This is a pleasant surprise. When did you get in?"

"About an hour ago. Randall Dumas will try to come later. R.C. sent the Falcon up for us. We heard about Tamara and thought you might need some help," Jim Takata said as they sat down. "You guys look like you need some fresh blood."

"Taking on these big boys won't be easy but most of us have done a lot of undercover work. We can find out some stuff for you," Brian said.

"Your timing is perfect. I have to go back to the plant on business. Maybe while I'm gone you can work with the team and get something started."

Michael laid out thoughts on their possible next move. He had to get to Vencenti and talk with him. The guys assured him they had some ways of making it happen. They would talk again when Michael returned.

Chapter 22

Enroute to the city Michael placed a number of calls to friends and business consultants he knew. He discussed his plans for Canon Aeronautics. They agreed to a nine AM meeting. He was glad the flight was a short one as time wasn't his ally. R.C. met him and they went straight back to the plant. He gathered the rest of his personal security team and he told them what was going on in the Bay Area. The team needed to be brought up to speed with who they might be dealing with. They also needed to be ready to move on a moments notice, fully armed. They kicked around some ideas and talked over the existing plans Michael had laid out. Going out of character to try and stay within the boundaries of the law was not an easy thing. They always made up their own rules of engagement as they saw fit. Leaving R.C. to finish up, Michael started to his office. He was stopped by C.J.

"I've been kinda worried about Stacy. How's she doing down there? I kinda feel that I should be down there too."

"I need you here with R.C."

"I know but I thought I was on the first line with the team, not in support."

Michael stopped, turned, and faced him.

"If I needed someone by my side I would pick you. I think you know that. I know you and Stacy talk everyday and I'm fine with that. What I can't figure out is why you haven't asked me how Tamara was doing?"

"Well Stacy told me she was hanging in there and a few minutes ago you said she was out of danger. I don't know what else you want from me."

"Nothing. Your job is to be R.C.'s shadow and you know what that entails. I trust no one else with that job. Now you tell me what's more important than that?"

"I'm sorry Mr. C, I guess I never looked at it quite like that before. Don't worry, I'll keep my end up."

Michael walked away. He still doesn't get it, Michael thought. Well, now that I've said something to him I feel a little better.

Michael talked to Marsha about what he was planning to do, company wise and though elated she was worried about him. He assured her he was fine but needed to make some major decisions for the future. When she left he called Tamara and talked with her for about a half hour. He told her he would be delayed tomorrow, but would see her around dinnertime. She understood. He called Stacy and gave her the list of the songs she wanted and asked her to purchase what they needed. He drove home and got some rest.

* *

The meeting started promptly at nine the next morning. Michael introduced everyone then began.

"Gentlemen, I am making a major decision in my life and this will affect all of you and those here at Aero. A few of you started with me back when we were scratching every week to keep our heads above water. We have come a long way. My health isn't as it used to be. Oh, I will live to have grandchildren but only if I ease the burden of full management and hours. I have thought about this for quite some time now and I have decided to change the operational parameters of the company. I have talked to several marketing and investment firms. You know these three men here and they will guide us through all the transitional issues. An employee stock ownership plan will be initiated immediately retroactive to our last fiscal year ending. I will remain Chairman of the Board and CEO but will limit my duties to final decision making. We carry a very light debt load and with the new contract and future forecasts, Aero will be very profitable. With our financial situation in the black we can rely on the newly passed laws to protect us from corporate raiders. You all have before you an outline for growth over the next ten years. I have instructions to divide ten blocks of stock between all of the employees according to time served. This is on top of what they may already own. With the new program, the employees will not have a decrease in their Social Security benefits and they'll be protected fully from seizure by personal future judgment creditors. At the close of the stock market Canon Aeronautics and its holdings are worth approximately two hundred thirty million dollars. That's it in a nutshell. Any questions?"

"Who will become president of operations?"

"That will be up to the board but I will be recommending you, Carl. Without you at my side all these years we wouldn't be where we are today."

"Thank you Michael. We all know you are the cornerstone of Canon Aeronautics and always will be."

"Carl, are you bucking for a raise?"

Everyone laughed as Michael patted him on the back.

"Now it's up to all of you to give the employees everything they've worked for. We will now take them all the way through their retirement and beyond. Thank you Gentlemen."

They all stood, applauded, and then lined up to shake his hand. Even the visitors were taken by his great generosity to his employees. They had never seen it done like this before. Marsha was in tears as the stenographer left the boardroom. Michael went and hugged her. He walked her back to his office and poured them some coffee.

"Michael, I've been with you from the start and I still can't believe what you've done for all of us. May I ask what you are going to get when everything is transferred?"

"I'll still have controlling stock and have a working relationship with the company in decision making. I'm doing this to protect not only the company but also the employees. I'll be around."

They finished their coffee and he gave her a big hug and kiss.

"Why didn't I marry you when I had the chance?"

"Oh you, you know why. I was already married. I'm going to miss you Michael."

It would be about a month before everything would be consummated. He looked at his watch then went down to see R.C. for any updates.

Chapter 23

The Falcon 2 arrived back at the World Airways Jetport around six thirty. Stacy took Michael back to the hospital. She handed him the package containing the CD player and the music. Chad Fox was on duty and Kennedy would relieve him for the late shift. Michael smiled and shut the door. He stopped and talked with Doctor Wallace for a moment to see if she knew of the prognosis. Nothing had changed so it was up to Michael.

She was so glad to see him she had tears in her eyes. He gave her the now standard carnation and the CD's. He sat on the bed next to her. She could see he was holding something back from her and asked him about it.

"The pressure can't be relieved anymore than it is. There's not another procedure they can try. In time we can only hope it will do it on it's own but for now they can't do anything more."

She gripped his arms very tightly as her eyes closed. She pulled him to her. He could see the total distress inside her as her hands got icy cold. They sat quietly for a few minutes as she moved her finger around his face.

"Can I ask you something?"

"Yes, anything."

"Will you help me to understand my new lifestyle? I mean therapy and the classes I'm going to need?"

"Only I will, nobody else," he said.

He bent down and held her. He let her mental emotions do what they wanted. He knew she had already figured it out and needed him to be honest with her. After about fifteen minutes she asked him what kind of songs he personally picked out for her.

"Actually, I had Stacy go shopping for me since I had to leave."

"I knew that," she said with a smile.

She looked at every CD and then asked him to pick one for her. He plugged in the player and set the volume. He looked through them all and opened one. He listened to the first few bars then let it rewind as he gave her the earphones.

"Think of me singing this to you," he said.

"You can't sing, but ok, I'll try."

She touched the play button then closed her eyes to enjoy whatever he picked out. He looked at the CD jacket that read: "*Be My Love*" by Mario Lanza. She pulled his hand to her mouth and kissed it without opening her eyes. When the song was over she turned it off and reached for him.

"I love you so much Michael, I'm sorry for messing everything up."

He held her tightly until the nurses came in an hour later. She was given a sedative.

Stacy picked him up and he told her of Tamara's condition. He held Stacy as her emotions too were beyond control. Soon he had her move over and he drove.

"Michael I am so weak I can't move. What you and she have to be going through has to be unimaginable. I'm so sorry."

"She knew before I told her and still she had a smile."

"That smile was for you. You're all she has in the world, she told me so."

"This might be cold to say but sometimes I think I'm too old for her," Michael commented. "She deserves someone younger, someone from her generation she can relate to…"

"Whoa, stop there just a minute. You listen to me Michael, that's a cop out and just down right bullshit. I can't believe you can think that way."

"It's just that…"

"If you're looking for an out then you've come to the wrong person Michael. Age doesn't have anything to do with her love for you. I'm sorry, but you've got this all wrong."

Michael looked at Stacy who he knew was distraught at his comment. After a quiet moment he reached across and mussed up her hair. "You're right, I'm a jerk."

"Hell, I'd marry you and I'm younger than Tam. How do you think that would go across?"

"Oh you would, would you?" Maybe I'll marry you both and really give society something to talk about."

Stacy broke out in a loud laugh, then commented, "You couldn't handle us both."

They stopped at a small diner and got some coffee. They both had to be under control completely before they met the team. They got back to the motel within the hour.

The team had indeed been working overtime with the addition of the Seattle four. Brian Hunt had set up a meeting between Michael and Vencenti for eight AM. Vencenti wasn't an easy sell. He would allow one bodyguard and a driver besides Michael to his mansion on the hill. They had found out a lot about Cattalo's operation. The thing Michael wanted to hear was Tony Sarino was still in town.

"We may have bitten more off here than we can chew," Michael said as Stacy handed him some coffee.

"There are still too many unknowns here. This could be our last hurrah but one thing is certain before we go down. You can carve up Cattalo and his organization any way you choose but Tony Sarino is mine and mine alone." Michael walked to the door and stopped. "I'll kill any man that cheats me out of Sarino."

He opened the door and went out slamming it behind him. Stacy told the team about Tamara's condition and a bomb thrown in amongst them couldn't have been worse. Now Tamara became the catalyst, the inner fuel and the purpose that bonded them all as one, again.

Chapter 24

The early morning rain had stopped as Mason drove the Lincoln up to the gates of Vencenti's mansion. He announced them and the gates opened. He drove slowly up the long drive and into the circle to the front of the dwellings. Armed men came up to the car and stood at both ends. Another man used a hand held metal detector to scan them both. Kennedy was allowed to keep his gun but the clip was removed and placed in his pocket. They were led up the stairs.

The house was old Victorian and was in better than average condition. Michael could see the inside was where the money had been spent, as it made one feel they had just gone back into another century. Kennedy was told to stay by the door and Michael followed the man for about fifty feet. One man was sitting but stood up when they approached.

"Michael Canon, sir," the man announced.

"Good morning Mr. Canon, I am Angelo Vencenti. Please be seated. Joseph, be kind enough to bring Mr. Canon's associate some coffee or whatever he would like."

"Thank you for seeing me on such short notice, Mr. Vencenti."

"Please, enough respect between two warriors, call me Angie. May I call you Michael?"

"Yes, thank you. You have the most beautiful home. I had almost forgotten how grand the past was. I'm taken by its aura."

"It's nice to see someone else knows how to appreciate fine workmanship. How can I help you?"

"We may be able to help each other," Michael said as a man approached.

"This is my advisor Mr. Garzi."

They both nodded their heads.

"I understand your gardens are magnificent this time of year," Michael said as he looked at Vencenti then Garzi.

Vencenti sensed what Michael was alluding to and stood up.

"Let take a walk and I'll show them to you. Mr. Garzi, we'll be back soon," Angelo said.

As they walked out Kennedy and one of Vencenti's men followed no closer than thirty feet behind them.

"I have followed you closely these past several years Michael, and I must say you have been quite busy."

Michael was stopped by his words as they walked.

"You know I came up from nothing but a dream and yes, I have done many things over my lifetime," Angelo began. "As I look back on them now, they are the reasons for my isolation here. No matter what I've done, when I raised my hand on Liberty Island as a boy, I have always been an American first. You were born with the oath and by your actions against the Colombians shows me how true you are also. Of this we can both be proud."

"I didn't realize what I've done has become common knowledge."

"There are a few of us left who have nothing better to do than search out the mysteries in life around us. Someone made a lot of foreigners disappear and I looked into it. Now, what can I do for you?"

"I am searching for Frank Cattalo and one of his people, Anthony Sarino."

"I know of them both."

"I met with Cattalo. He agreed to give me Sarino then made a hit on me and my associates."

"May I ask why you want this Sarino, Michael?" he inquired as they sat down across from each other in a circular garden.

"It's a story with an unhappy ending."

"I would like to hear it Michael."

Michael told him the story as he figured it happened. Vencenti listened intently and watched Michael's eyes. Michael left nothing out of the scenario.

"Yes, I read it in the newspaper. My heart went out to the woman who died."

"The woman was my fiancée and she didn't die, though she is wishing she had. She is paralyzed from the waist down."

Vencenti closed his eyes, slowly put his fingers to his lips and said a prayer.

"Anthony Sarino pulled the trigger, I have it on tape."

"Michael, if I could give her my legs I would. Please feel my heart and the sympathy that's in it, for both of you."

"For the moment my sources have been unable to locate either of them and that's the reason I am here, for your help if you can give it," Michael said.

Vencenti raised his hand in a small circle. Michael looked back over his shoulder to see a servant bringing a tray of drinks. Angie took one and motioned for Michael to have one. Angelo took a pill from a small silver tin and swallowed it with some water.

"Michael I am torn between honor and blood here. What you ask may be impossible for me to give. Anthony Sarino is my Godson."

Michael just sat there and looked at him.

"Angie, I want to thank you for seeing me. You know I must do what I feel is right. Are you going to walk back up to the house?"

"No, thank you for asking. I do feel in my heart for you and her. I am glad you came."

Michael turned and walked several steps then stopped. He turned and looked at Vencenti.

"Mr. Vencenti, do we have a problem between us?"

"No Michael, there is no problem."

Michael walked back to the car. They drove out of the front gates and back to the motel. He was no closer to finding Sarino than before, but he did learn a lesson in life.

Chapter 25

Angelo Vencenti came up through the doings and preaching of the old Philadelphia guard of the La Cosa Nostra. His father, a long time soldier, died protecting his crime boss in a mini family war. Not able to go any further within the east coast family he served, he migrated west. Offered a position within the main San Francisco family establishment, it was alleged Vencenti was detrimental in the elimination of Jimmy Pesiero, one of the street bosses in Oakland. At the height of Vencenti's rise he was deep into California produce. At one time he controlled nearly eighty percent of the olive industry.

He was now a man in his late sixties and if he had a weakness over the years, it was women. There was a stable of models and teens he had at his disposal through several of the hotels in the area. He wasn't lying in bed alone too often.

He would have gladly given all this up when he came to California had one special women stepped his way. Samantha Lyndon Connerly had taken his heart twenty years earlier. Shortly after he came to the area he befriended Samantha, who was the fiancée of one of the up and coming prosecuting attorneys. Matthias Connerly had the eye of the highest local and federal authorities and made a name for himself through high profile trials. His uncontrollable temper carried over into his personal life and Samantha, whose marriage to him was politically arranged, suffered. He physically beat her when things went wrong in his job and this brought Samantha and Angelo closer together. Through an arrangement they both set up, Angelo and Samantha would spend a day or a weekend together when they could.

As Vencenti rose up in power, Connerly stayed on him to a point that Vencenti was thinking of removing him from office permanently. Because of his love for Samantha he honored her request not to do it. She was sixty now and though they were not as sexually active as in past days, just being together quantified their reasons for living.

Chapter 26

Michael went to the hospital to have lunch with Tamara. He told Stacy to pick him up in two hours and to call Sommers to tell him the clock was ticking. He would know what it meant.

Sommers came to the hospital and met with Michael in the hallway. Because of the action taken to report her as dead, Michael sheltered her from all questions about the shooting. Sommers now asked Michael for permission to allow Tamara to look at some mug shots to see if she recognized any of the possible shooters that night. He said he could and stayed with her as she looked the photos over. She identified Sarino as the closest one to her but was not sure of the others as it happened so fast. Sommers thanked her then Michael walked with him to the hall. Sommers gave him slips containing the location of Cattalo and suspected business holdings he might have.

"I will see what I can do to have Sarino picked up. In the meantime I want to know what you're doing at all times. You have to work with me Michael."

Michael told him of his meeting with Vencenti which totally caught him by surprise.

"Michael you're going to get yourself killed. You can't just go visit someone like Vencenti without putting yourself on his list. We can't protect you if you keep going the way you are."

"You are going to protect me? Tamara is the only one that needs protection and you can't do that. You just help me get Sarino and I'm out of here. You can have the others," Michael said, then walked back into Tamara's room.

Chapter 27

Majestic Imports
San Leandro, California

Majestic Imports was a medium-sized auto dealership specializing in foreign cars. It was a legitimate business from the showroom out. Behind it was another business that included acquiring hard to find vehicles and boats then exporting them before they could be traced by the authorities. Cattalo wasn't afraid to hijack a load of high priced commodes coming into the area and shipping them off to Mexico or Canada. There he could reap the higher profits for himself.

The last of the men Cattalo had hired from around the country had arrived. He greeted them in the triple-wide modular home in the rear of the property he used for his main office. They poured some drinks and he gave them a rough overview of what they had been brought in for. Sal Danza, one of his street triggermen walked in carrying four boxes of pizzas followed by his girlfriend carrying fried chicken and beer.

"Hi Frankie, where do you want these?" she asked.

"Right here on the table Candice, where do you think?"

As they ate one of the men threw a chicken leg and missed the plate of scraps. It fell on the floor. He kept on eating. Candice asked him if he was going to pick it up. He looked at her and kept eating. She made an off the wall comment about a pig and the guy stood up.

"Hey, knock it off. Candice get the hell out of here," Frank said.

"Why do I have to leave, he's the slob."

"Sal, get her out of my sight. She doesn't need to be here, we're talking business."

"But Frankie, she's one of us. She didn't mean anything by that," Sal said looking at her.

Frank pulled her out of her chair and shoved her towards the kitchen. "Go clean up the kitchen or something."

"That's not right Frankie, you've done well by her," Sal said as he headed to the kitchen.

Just then Tony Sarino came in. He had been gone for several days on business.

"I was just telling the guys how you took care of that little thing at the Sheridan."

He got several "atta boys" from a few at the table. They continued to talk.

"You know Candice, you can't keep opening your mouth like that around people. Frankie doesn't like that," Sal said as he held her in the kitchen. "I mean he likes you and all but you always talk when you shouldn't."

"Well he's not so smart."

"Oh no, he is really smart and we're gonna do right by him, you'll see."

"Oh really, they screwed up that thing at the hotel, now that was really smart," she said breaking away from him.

"Hey, keep your voice down, he'll hear you."

"I don't care if he does. If he's so smart he'd know that the woman didn't die. So see he ain't so smart."

"Candice, lower your voice, I mean…"

The door to the kitchen slammed open and Frank stood there looking at her for a moment.

"What do you mean she didn't die?"

"I didn't mean anything by it. I was just talkin', you know?"

Frank grabbed her by the arm and pulled her back into the room with the other guys. "Tell me what you said."

"Come on Frankie, she was just talking shit, she doesn't know," Sal said.

Frank pulled out his automatic and pointed it at Sal. "If you say another word Sally I'm gonna blow your head off. Now, talk to me Candice."

"Ok, ok. Well, I was moved up to the sixth floor to help out and I asked about this one lady who always had a guy outside her door, you know, like a bodyguard or something."

"Get on with it," Tony said impatiently.

"Well I hear she was the one that got shot in an escalator or elevator or something like that. Anyway, they told everybody she was dead."

"You fucking idiot," Frank yelled to Tony. "You said you had taken care of her."

"I did, the news said she was dead. What was I supposed to think?"

"You didn't think; that's the problem. Ok Candice, why is she still there?"

"Oh Frankie, it's so sad. She's paralyzed. She can't move, isn't that sad?"

Frank threw up his hands, walked to the window and looked out.

"I'll go back and take care of her," Tony said as he poured another drink.

"You can't take care of it, weren't you listening to her? She's guarded around the clock, cops probably."

"No, they're not cops. I think they're private guys," Candice said.

Frank walked to her and she started to back up as he put his hands on her arms and pulled her into him. "You did well. Maybe I'm not so smart. I'm sorry I yelled at you."

"Oh, that's all right Frankie, I do talk too much sometimes."

"When do you work there again?" Frankie asked.

"Tonight. I should be going to get ready."

"Candice, you could do me a real big favor."

"What kind of favor?"

"I want you to go and see the woman and do something for me. It's worth a thousand to me."

"Just to go see her?"

"We can't go there because of the guards but you can go in. I want you to put something in her medicine bag for me."

"Oh no Frankie, I couldn't do anything like that again. The old lady was one thing. She was dying anyway."

"How much do you love Sal?"

"A lot, we're gonna get married as soon as he says."

"If this woman gets out she's gonna testify she saw Sal with the others and they're going to come after him. We don't want that now do we?"

"No. Do I really get the money too?"

Frankie reached in his pocket, counted out ten one hundred dollar bills and gave them to her. She tried to take them but he didn't let go. "You have to do it tonight. Tony will fix a syringe for you. Just go in, do it, and come out. Nobody will know."

Chapter 28

The team had moved to another motel and would do frequently from now on. Michael split up the team to do some surveillance on the places Sommers had listed. Stacy dropped Michael off at the hospital and returned to the Inn.

"This could get habit forming having dinner with you every night," Michael said as they brought her dinner and an extra one for him.

"I am getting to enjoy the habit but how come yours always looks better than mine?"

"Yours is home cooked and mine is catered."

"Oh really," she said with a big smile.

"My doctor back home prescribed this for me just like doctor Wallace says that's what you should eat."

"No he didn't, you're making that up," Tamara said as she reached for some of his peaches and cottage cheese.

They both laughed then shared each other's food.

"Michael, I'm sorry for the things I said the other day. I am trying so hard to accept all of this."

"You have nothing to apologize about. We are going to work this out together, agreed?"

"You're the boss," she said with a smile.

"I hear they are going to move you to the fifth floor to a nicer room so they can begin your therapy," Michael said.

"Tomorrow. I am still kind of scared. I don't know if I can do this."

"No, I think the word is *we* can do this, don't you?"

"This is so new to me. I'll do us both proud, you'll see."

They had now seen so much of each other; Michael was running out of things to talk about that related to them personally without going into her therapy and beyond. She liked the music but gave him another short list of other songs she would like to have. Around eight the nurses came in to prepare her for the night. Michael went back to the motel.

Chapter 29

About a quarter to ten, Stacy walked in the hospital with Kennedy. They got to the sixth floor nurses station and Kennedy immediately started a conversation with Catherine who had just come on.

"Candice, why don't you go ahead and I'll catch up with you," Catherine said as Kennedy had brought her a small box of chocolates.

"Ok," Candice said as she started up the hall behind Stacy.

"Paul, I'll only be a minute, I have to go to the little girl's room. Go and harass Shawn."

Paul saw Kennedy down at the nurse's station and headed his way. He said hi to the young aide passing him and kept walking. Candice stopped as she got to Tamara's door and looked around. The two guys were at the nurse's desk so she pushed open the door. Tamara was sleeping soundly. She walked over to the tree holding the two liquid medicine bags of fluids going into Tamara's arm.

Stacy walked out of the ladies room and headed back to the nurse's area. As she approached Tamara's room she could see Candice standing next to the bed opening a small black box. Stacy walked faster as a hypodermic needle came out of it and Candice put the box back in her pocket. Stacy hit the door hard as Candice reached for the tubes on the tree. Stacy lunged at her. Candice swiped at her with the syringe but missed. Stacy spun her around and grabbed Candice's right wrist. Candice struggled wildly kicking the bed which woke Tamara. Stacy raised Candice's arm up then brought it back into Candice's stomach with everything she had. Candice began to shake violently then fell to the floor, as Kennedy, Paul, and two of the nurses rushed in.

"Call Michael," Stacy said as one of the nurses bent down and checked the neck of the aide.

"She's dead."

Michael called Sommers and they arrived at the same time. They had moved Candice out of the room and Stacy was sitting with Tamara. Doctor Wallace said they were doing a toxicology report on the contents of the syringe and would know very soon. Michael held Tamara as Kennedy and Wallace cleared everyone away from the area.

"Michael, do they know I'm here?"

"How they found out I don't know but we're getting you out right now. I need to talk to Wallace. Are you gonna be all right?"

"Yes, have Stacy stay with me."

He kissed her then motioned for Stacy to come back in.

Wallace took Michael and Sommers to his office.

"I need to call the police, its standard procedure," Wallace said.

"My authority supercedes theirs and I'm classifying this as a federal matter. Michael what do you want to do?"

"I want to move her out of here. Is there another facility you know of that you can treat her at?" Michael asked Wallace.

There was a knock at the door. The floor nurse came in, handed the doctor a sheet of paper, and then left.

"Potassium cyanide," Wallace said as he handed it to Sommers. "Whoever it was knew how to use it."

"I need a place to put her or I'll take her back to Nevada," Michael said.

"Let's move her to Park View. They're our sister hospital across town that just opened this month. She'll be safe there."

"I want information on the dead girl. Maybe we can find out something," Sommers said.

"What about her, I need to file a report."

"List her death as an accident. You know, accidentally stuck herself with a needle. It must happen all the time," Sommers answered.

"Why aren't I surprised to hear that coming from a fed?" Michael commented as they left the room.

Tamara was quietly moved from the hospital to Park View under the fully armed escort of the team. Within two hours Sommers had an answer from his inquiry of Candice.

"Arrested for petty theft and suspected of being an accessory in a jewelry store robbery but never convicted. Known associates included Peter Batti and Salvatore Danza. They both work for Cattalo," Sommers said. "We could pick them up but they'd be out in an hour. We can't prove they sent the girl even though we know they did."

Chad Fox asked to take the watch until dawn and Michael agreed.

On Michael's inquiry regarding full-time nurses Wallace suggested Catherine, who took care of Tamara now, and two other part time nurses he knew to work full time for Michael. He would handle it with the hospital. Kennedy had no problem with that when Michael told him about Catherine.

"I'm sorry for what happened, I am trying to keep you safe and it looks like I'm falling short there," Michael said as he sat down with her.

"Please don't say that my darling, I couldn't be safer. I know things happen but I'm fine and I don't want you to worry about that," she said then kissed him. "Actually, I feel like the First Lady with all this round the clock protection."

"Yeah, how do you know about that?"

"Oh I've been watching some TV and she was in the hospital too for a checkup. There is something you can do for me though."

"Anything, you just ask."

"She had some pretty good-looking bodyguards. The ones you give me look like they always want to beat up somebody."

"Oh do they now," he said as he put his arms around her and blew against her neck.

She giggled and tried to bite his ear. "You just wait until I get out of here and you're in big trouble Mister."

"That'll be soon. Listen, I've gotta go. You try and get some sleep and leave the bodyguards alone. I'm doing the best with what I've got," he said with a smile then kissed her the way she liked.

When he got back to the motel they all assembled in one room and Michael wanted a full report. Paul laid out what he knew happened.

"Paul, I know you haven't been with us long enough to know how we do things but…"

"Michael, it's nobody's fault but mine. I sent him down to the nurse's station thinking I would have been out of the bathroom quicker, but it didn't turn out that way. I'm to blame, nobody else."

Michael lit a cigarette and the room got quiet.

"Paul, you and Brian take the morning watch. Stacy, if you hadn't taken so long in the ladies she would probably be dead right now. Things happen for a reason. You all did your jobs well. I think we had better go on the offensive soon or it's only going to get worse."

Paul thanked him for having trust in him. Michael and the team spent the next couple of hours looking over all the Intel the surveillance teams had gathered.

Chapter 30

A black limousine stopped at the gates of the Vencenti mansion. The gates opened and it proceeded to the house. Tony Sarino got out followed by two of Vencenti's men.

"Antonio, it's good to see you, please sit."

"Hi Uncle Angelo, is everything all right. You're not sick or anything, are you?"

"No I am fine. It's you that I am worried about."

"I feel fine."

"Antonio, you have gotten yourself into a lot of trouble. Tell me about the Sheridan hotel."

"I go there once in a while."

"Antonio, slow down and select you answers very carefully. You know what I'm talking about."

"Well, the boys and I had a little trouble but nothing to worry about. Why all the questions?"

"A man has come to town to find you. A very important man. He knows you were involved with the shooting and he's looking for you."

"What man? Should I be scared of a single man? Hey, I'm from the family and we're not afraid of any man," Tony said as he stood up. "He doesn't scare me, I'll handle him."

"Antonio, sit down, show some respect!" Angie yelled.

"Ok I'm sitting. I meant no disrespect Uncle Angelo."

"You must go away. Maybe I can handle this but I don't know how yet."

"You sound like you're afraid of him."

"Yes, and you should be too," Angie yelled as he slapped his hand on the table. "He is the most dangerous man on the face of God's earth once he's provoked."

Tony sipped some water. "What do you suggest I do?"

"Go away someplace. Denver, Phoenix, Miami, anywhere, but stay there until I call you."

Tony stood up. "Sure Uncle Angelo, I'll call you when I get someplace."

Tony walked back to the limousine and they drove off.

Chapter 31

Michael returned from the hospital just as Brian Hunt drove up. They went inside.

"You were right, Sarino went to visit with his uncle, or was brought there. They talked on the patio then he left. I don't think the uncle looked too happy with the kid. How'd you know?"

"Obvious reasoning. Where did he go from there?"

"They took him to a place called Majestic Imports. That's one of the places on our list."

"Good we're getting somewhere. We need a surveillance team on it."

"Already done. Jim and Arron are spelling each other."

"Good work," Michael said as he scanned the list of places Cattalo had.

* * * * * * * * * * * * * * * * * * * *

Majestic Imports
San Leandro, California

"What the hell was that all about?" Frank asked Tony as he came in the office.

"Oh it was nothing. My uncle just wanted to talk a little, that's all."

"Level with me. I can't have you into anything that will jeopardize what we have planned."

"He said there's someone in town looking for me. It had something to do with that hotel shooting. My uncle, he worries too much."

"Well worry about this. Candice didn't come back this morning from the hospital and she's nowhere to be found. Sal and Pete have been out looking for her all morning. I don't like this. I called the hospital as a reporter and they said they had no woman from any hotel shooting. I don't know what to believe. Now it's your Goddamned problem and you better deal with it. Find Candice too."

"Hell, she probably did what you asked then skipped town. You paid her enough."

"Maybe, but I doubt it."

Sarino took two of the new men and left. They drove over to Berkeley to the Continental Tire and Recap and parked on the side of the building.

Arron drove up slowly and parked across the street. He took a magnetic transceiver from his shirt pocket and activated it. He got out of his car and walked over to the now vacated sedan and placed it under the inside portion of the frame below the front door. He went back to his car and waited.

"How's it look for tonight?" Tony asked one of his men when he got inside.

"Right on schedule, like you figured. The truck will be coming in through Sacramento full of new Pirelli's and we'll have them out of here by tomorrow night."

"Good," Tony said as he turned and walked out.

The three got back in the car and headed out. Arron had his earplug in and listened as he followed them at a long distance.

"I am personally going to make sure this is done right. We're going to follow them tonight. That truckload of tires is worth its weight in gold, my gold," Tony said.

Chapter 32

Michael called Sommers with the information Arron had received and Sommers said he would act on it. As much as Michael wanted Tony Sarino, he had to give Sommers and the authorities a shot at taking them down. Highjacking carried one of the stiffest penalties in the federal courts. Michael told Sommers if he didn't make the arrest with this opportunity then it would be his turn. Sommers didn't like it but agreed, for now. The agency was more intent on going after Vencenti. A warrant for Sarino alone wouldn't play out even though he was present at the hotel. They still couldn't prove he was the actual shooter. To take down Cattalo was a better prize in their move on local organized crime. Their job was to get all of them or nothing.

Since they didn't know the origin of the truck Sommers could only wait and shadow Sarino and his men.

Sommers sat in his car beside another federal team in the Rainbow Food parking lot kitty-corner from the Continental Tire warehouse. Stacy brought the SUV up next to them. Sommers got out and got into the Escalade.

"I hate waiting," Sommers said as Stacy handed him a paper cup of coffee. "Thanks Stacy."

"You've got to learn patience Clay. Think of it as not wanting to go home because your mother-in-law hasn't left yet," Michael said as they watched the warehouse.

"I don't have a mother-in-law so that won't fly."

"Oh Clay, work with me here. I'm just trying to put a little fun in your life."

"They're leaving," Arron said. "He's talking to someone on his cell. He must have somebody following the truck."

Sommers got out.

Michael watched as three cars left the rear of the warehouse and passed by them heading for I80. Sommers and the other car headed out to follow them.

"All we can do now is to have a little patience," Michael said as he sat back in the passenger seat. "I'll buy if someone goes in and gets some donuts."

* *

Sommers had received an earpiece from Arron and he listened to Sarino's idle chatter as they drove. Just above Pinole they had to pass Sarino who slowed down and pulled over. A quarter mile ahead they passed a state rest area and figured the highjacking would take place in the southbound rest area opposite them. They stopped in the northbound rest area and waited. In about ten minutes they saw the semi signal and enter the southbound rest area. Several other cars exited and all but one went into the passenger side of the rest area. One of Sommer's men kept his video camera going as they watched the truck driver get out and go into the washroom. The car following stopped next to the truck and two men went into the washroom. Shortly they came out and one jumped into the truck. The car headed out followed by the semi.

"They're heading in. Is the assault team in position?" Sommers asked on the radio.

"We're all set here."

Sommers waited thirty seconds then proceeded to the crossover and headed back south. Just ahead of them they could see Sarino's car use the median turn-around and headed back south away from them. They backed off, keeping Sarino in sight. Traffic was heavier than usual.

"We've just passed El Cerrito. They should be very close to you anytime. Assault one you have the ball," Sommers said.

"We roger that."

Sommers put his hand to his earpiece. "Shit, he's pulling over. Team two keep moving to the next exit and come back."

They passed Sarino's car pulled over at the southbound Harrison Exit and kept going to the next turn-around before the bridge.

As he approached the northbound Harrison Exit off ramp Sommers could see that Sarino's car was nowhere to be seen. As they exited I80 north there were six cars ahead of them stopped for the southbound freight that was just going by. From that location there was no other quick way to get around the train so they waited. It was eight minutes before they crossed the tracks and arrived at Continental Tire. The assault team had seized the entire shipment and two of Cattalo's men were killed in a brief shootout. Sommers called Michael who had watched the entire assault. He told him Sarino had eluded them.

"You had your chance, now it's ours," Michael commented.

"Wait, let's get together and talk about this," Sommers said, then realized Michael had hung up.

The bust was a good one for the authorities. The report Sommers received the next morning showed the company was owned and operated by an overseas holding company. Frank Cattalo's name was not listed in the report.

Chapter 33

The newer hospital was more to Michael's liking as he walked through to the elevators. He got off on the fourth floor, turned right and followed the signs that read, PHYSICAL THERAPY. Doctor Wallace was on his way across town but wanted to monitor Tamara's first day in therapy. She waved at Michael as he stood by the doctor. Two therapists were going to slowly build up her upper body and arms. They watched the readings on the monitors and Wallace said she would do fine. After twenty minutes the session was over.

"Good morning my darling," Tamara said as they pulled the monitor's wire pads from her skin. "I have so many of these things on me I think if you look in my eyes you can get a cable channel."

Michael laughed and gave her a kiss. He watched the attendants closely at how they handled her. He would have to do the same thing when she finally was able to leave.

"I have put together some tapes that I think would interest you in caring for her," Jon said as he handed the chart back to the therapist. "It's basically how to lift and move her, bathing techniques, that kind of thing. There is one on understanding the mental aspect also. I'll bring them over this afternoon."

"I worry about you staying safe when you're not here Michael. I worry about losing you."

"I am covered around the clock just like you. I'll think twice before I do something, ok?"

She smiled. "Can I ask you a question?"

"Sure, anything."

"When we leave here where are we going?"

Michael thought for a moment.

"That's all right, I shouldn't have asked that," she added.

"No, it's not that. I'm wondering the same thing. I put my place up for sale and I think they have a buyer. We may both be homeless. I'll think on it and we'll talk more about it."

"Ok. Listen, if you're going to be here for a little while longer, why don't you go have a smoke and send Stacy in. I want to do some girl talk."

"You mean I can't listen?"

"Go. I may be armed so don't mess with me mister."

"You're a tough woman," he said as he kissed her.

Chapter 34

Frank Cattalo sat in his Lexus and looked at his watch. He was a few minutes early for his appointment so he watched as people parked and walked into the main entrance to the mall. His eye caught a glimpse of a white Cadillac limousine approaching. It stopped two parking spots from him. The driver got out and stood by the rear door as Frank got out and started walking towards him. As he neared the limo the driver opened the door and Frank got in.

"Talk to me Frank," the man next to him said.

"The first part of the plan is in place. My man, DeSeno, is inside and ready to proceed when we tell him."

"This weekend I've worked it out to be away. I think that is when this should all take place. The time will be up to you."

"I understand," Frank said.

"One other thing Frank, the way you handled the hotel matter is an embarrassment. Word has it the feds are looking into it. An arrest warrant was requested for your boy Sarino regarding the hotel incident. I was able to stop the action. I think you had better put him on ice. The last thing you need is to screw our deal up then have to deal with me. We need to have our operation go without any problems."

"Don't worry, I am on top of this," Frank said as he got out of the limousine.

The limo driver got in and drove away.

Cattalo sat in his car for a few minutes thinking about their conversation. Not only had Tony put him in an embarrassing situation, he lost the entire tire shipment to the feds at Continental Tire. Up until this all happened his operation and plans were going well and right on schedule. This next phase of his plan to bring down Vencenti from the mountain could have no mistakes. He knew his own life depended on it being carried out to the letter. He headed to the Crown Point marina in Alameda.

* *

Brad Hunt had Frank Cattalo under constant surveillance. Following him to the marina he parked and watched Cattalo leave his car. Cattalo headed down to one of the big yachts on the end. He could see two men standing guard, one at each end of the yacht on the dock. Cattalo was searched at the gangway then boarded. Brian called Michael.

"The yacht is called April Rain out of San Diego. One of the workers here said it belonged to someone named Lappet. One other thing, Cattalo just met with someone important. You might want to check out the license number."

Brian read the number to him.

"Nice work Brian, Chad is on his way to relieve you. Call us if Cattalo leaves before Chad gets there."

Michael called Sommers and asked about Lappet. He also requested the license plate be checked through the DMV.

"I don't know how you find out all these things but you are getting into deeper water every minute," Sommers stated.

"That's the story of my life, now what about Lappet?"

"He's the head of the second largest crime family in the area. Now you're not going to go do something stupid are you?"

"Stop worrying, I'm just trying to put this puzzle together. You know me I'm the curious type," Michael answered.

"That is the scary part. I am getting to know you. Call me before you do anything rash," Sommers ordered, then hung up.

Michael kicked his thoughts around with a few members of the team. He couldn't figure the connection between a second rate street boss like Cattalo and someone big like Lappet. Sarino was Vencenti's Godson yet he worked for Cattalo. Brian called back to say Chad had arrived to relieve him. Cattalo left the yacht five minutes later. They both followed Cattalo back to his dealership then Brian headed back to the motel.

As Brian arrived, Michael had received some interesting information from Erickson on Lappet.

Leo Lappet came out from the east coast to replace his ailing brother as head of the number two crime family in the area. They were strong into the unions. Nothing came or went through the docks without them having a piece of it. Erickson also mentioned very few arrests had been made since he took over. Lappet has been suspected of dealings in gunrunning, drugs, and murder but nothing had ever been proven.

"Find Johnnie Lima, we need to have another talk with him," Michael ordered.

Brian called to the two units in the field and relayed Michael's message. Within the hour they found out where

Lima would be. Michael, Mason, and Jim left to pay him a visit.

They headed downtown to a comedy club called the Noisy Parrot.

"What's this?" Michael asked, pointing to the side of Jim's boot.

"They're small throwing knives. I use to be pretty good with them but after I saw Tamara's skills, I went back to school. I've studied hard these past months. I feel better now with them."

"You've done well Jim, I'm glad you came down."

The line was fairly long at the door but the hundred Michael gave the burly door attendant got them in. Tonight was voice impersonator night. Not seeing Lima as they walked around the outside of the large main room, they went to the bar. Michael listened to the end of a song sung by a man with a very easy listening but dynamic style. He applauded as the song ended.

"He's very good," Michael said to Jim standing next to him.

"I don't think the old songs do well in a place like this. The people here barely clapped."

The next performer had to be a local as a lot of people stood up and applauded her as she was introduced. The gal, in her mid to late twenties was performing something by Streisand. Michael applauded when she finished as she had done the original artist proud. Mason spotted Lima at the end of the other bar across the room. The three split up in hopes Lima wouldn't see them coming and try to run. Michael walked slowly through the crowd and right up to Lima. He saw Michael and turned to his right to leave. His face buried into Mason's chest.

"Please, I can't do this again. Leave me alone," he said as Mason turned him around.

They walked to an empty table to the right of the bar and put Lima in a chair. Mason and Jim stood with their backs to them and looked out at the crowd.

"Johnnie, I need to pick your brain one more time," Michael said.

"Hey, I'm still hurting from you throwing me out of the truck. Are you gonna do something to me again?"

"What did they say to you when you went back to the tattoo joint?"

"Oh man, they really felt for me, you know?"

"See, if we hadn't done that you'd probably be dead."

"You're probably right, but we aren't going for another ride, are we?"

"No. Listen to me. What do you know about Leopold Lappet and his organization? Tell me straight and there will be some big money in it for you."

"What kind of money?"

"Four figures, but that's if it's the information I want," Michael said as he lit a cigarette.

Johnnie laid out all he knew of Lappet's operation. He even speculated on his after dark activity on the docks.

"What's Cattalo's interest in Lappet?"

"I guess that's where Frank gets his drugs. They come in from Mexico."

"What kind of drugs?"

"Ludes, ampheds, cocaine, heroin patches, that kind of thing."

"Are you talking about LIFE patches?"

"Yeah, I've seen 'em."

"Any word on when he might be expecting another shipment?"

"Are you sure you're gonna pay four figures, you're not just saying that?" Johnnie asked as he reached for one of Michael's cigarettes.

Michael pulled a money roll from his pocket and counted out five one-hundred dollar bills. He slid them over to Johnnie, and then said, "You can double this right now. When and where is his next shipment coming in?"

"Hey, all I now right now is they use pier 17 off of King Street. They come in north of the ferry route by the Bay Bridge."

"When?"

"Sometime this weekend but don't know right now, and that's the truth."

Michael wrote down his cell number and gave it to him.

"You tell me a time and I'll double this," Michael said. "You walk out on me and you'll get a ride in my plane. You'll also get a great view of the Bay area as you fall from it. Do we understand?"

Johnnie looked into Michael's eyes. "Yes sir, you don't have to say it again."

Michael got up and walked past the kid and the team followed. As they got halfway to the front door Michael stopped and looked at the stage. The people were barely applauding the next performer. He was the same man they saw when they came in. He was nice looking and in his late twenties. He removed the microphone from the stand. The spotlight centered on the man and the taped background music began. Michael knew the song and he wanted to hear his voice again. The song was, *Be My Love* and the man sung it as if Lanza was doing it himself. It sent chills down Michael's back as he watched the performer put his all into it. The song might have been too heavy a number for the in-crowd as Jim had mentioned. The applause he received wasn't even half of what the others had gotten. As he left the stage Michael and the team went backstage. Michael asked where he might find the man and the stage manager pointed out his room. The door was partially opened so Jim went in first. There were several other music star look-alikes walking around. He saw their man in the corner just sitting and staring into the mirror.

"I enjoyed your performance," Michael said as he came up behind him.

"You're probably the only one," the man said without turning around.

"I'm Michael Canon and you are?"

"Larry Courier," he said as he stood up.

"I just wanted to tell you I thought I was listening to the real thing."

Larry brought another chair up and Michael sat down.

"What brought you to choose Lanza as a model?" Michael asked.

"I guess I want him to live forever as his music does. I've spent a great deal of time learning about the man and really try my absolute best to keep his sound going."

"Well, you have one fan. You seem very down though, are you having a problem with someone here?"

"Nothing I haven't lived with for a while. I can't compete with the rock music of today and most of the clubs prefer them now. The stuff that's out there isn't singing, its yelling and blaring amplifiers."

"Have you heard of Glamour Tours?"

"Who hasn't, but you have to know someone there to get in. Wait a minute, are you with them?"

Michael smiled and said he wasn't.

"Hey Courier, get your ass going. You have another spot to do so let's move it," they heard as a big guy in an undershirt came into the room and approached them.

"Mason," Michael said as he was almost on them.

Mason stopped the man. "He's busy right now."

"Who the hell are you? Get out of my way," the guy said as he went to move Mason aside.

Mason grabbed the persistent loud mouth and threw him about six feet into the table behind him. He went crashing to the floor. He got back up just as another bruiser his size came through the door. They both headed their way but this time Jim and Mason pulled their automatics. The two froze in their tracks.

"Sit down and shut up," Mason said.

The two sat on the floor. Everyone else left quickly. They returned their automatics to their holsters and stood there looking at the two men.

"I'm sorry for that," Michael said. "My men don't like for me to be interrupted when I'm with someone."

"Are you someone I should be worrying about?"

Michael smiled and told him no.

"You mentioned something about Glamour Tours, do you know somebody there?"

"I know one of the producers and a couple of the booking agents. They might want to talk to you," Michael said.

"By the time I get out of here, hopefully in one piece, I wouldn't have enough to buy Band-Aids. You better get out of here. I'm going to hear about this later, big time."

"What will it take to get you out of hock with them?"

"They advanced me three hundred for the next two weeks and that's not going very far. Kratsman will make me work three weeks to pay off the interest."

Michael told Jim to have someone get this Kratsman. One of the guys on the floor jumped up and headed out.

"I think we're all in big trouble now. He's not one you want to mess with," Larry said as he sipped some water.

A well-dressed man surrounded by two bigger guys than Mason, walked in.

"You don't come in here and start throwing your weight around. Who are you and what do you want?"

Michael stood up as Mason motioned for them to stop about ten feet from them.

"How much does he owe you?"

"More than you can pay. How much is his life worth to you?"

Just then the door behind them opened loudly and they heard the sound of a shotgun bringing a shell into the breach.

"You see, you don't come into my club and give orders."

Michael and the three just stood still. Larry backed up by his dressing table.

"I think you ought to forget him and start wondering how much it's gonna cost you to leave in one piece," Kratsman said, as he walked up to Michael.

"How about your life for his?" a voice behind them said.

They looked around and saw Scott standing behind the shotgun wielding man holding a .357 magnum against his ear. The door they originally came in opened and there stood the Larch brothers with their .45's drawn. Kratsman's expression changed as he backed up with his men.

"I asked you a question before. I'll not ask it again," Michael said.

"Hey, I guess it's about three hundred but let's not worry about it."

Michael pulled out three hundred dollars and stuffed it into Kratsman's shirt pocket. "If I ever get word this man has even a scratch on him there will be no place you can hide. How about a receipt?"

"A receipt, sure. Who do I make it out to?" Kratsman asked.

Michael told Larry to get his things. He did so within a minute. They walked by Kratsman and Michael said, "Make it out to Angelo Vencenti."

As Michael and Larry went through the door he looked back to see Kratsman sitting down with his head in his hands. They walked out of the club to the waiting Escalade.

"Scotty, what are you doing here?" Michael said as he hugged him.

"I missed you Boss."

Handshakes and hugs went around to Dawson and Brandon and then they headed back to the motel. Larry rode with Michael.

"I thought we were all dead back there Mr. Canon. Thanks for getting me out of there."

"You have a car or things here?"

"No, just what I have here. I was paid up through tomorrow at the place I was staying.

"I'm known to be a good judge of character Larry. We all get stuck sometimes and need a hand to get going again. I think you were stuck back there. You have a God gifted talent, one that I appreciate. I'm going to call my friends at Glamour and tell them you'll be by to see them. If that's not what you have in mind for your life, now is the time to speak up."

"I'm very grateful to all of you but can I ask you a personal question?"

"Sure anything."

"Are you guys with the, you know, mafia or something?"

They all couldn't help but laugh.

"No Larry, we are just a bunch of guys that do good things from time to time. Of course one day I might call you and ask for a favor. Now, what do you say?"

"What can I say but yes?"

Stacy and Arron had bought some food and they all indulged. They laughed at the look on Kratsman's face when Scott cocked his magnum.

"How did you find us?" Mason asked.

"R.C. put a micro-chip in your cell phone. We just zeroed in on the signal. Since you weren't in the lounge you had to be backstage. It was easy," Scott answered.

Larry couldn't figure out why everybody around him was armed, but he didn't care. He just knew his luck was changing.

Michael took Larry over to where Ernie was sitting. He explained that Ernie would fly him to the city where he could meet his friends at Glamour Tours. He gave him a thousand dollars to get him started. Larry was choked up as he shook Michael's hand.

"Anytime you ever need me Mr. Canon, you just call me and I'll be there," Larry said as he said goodbye and left with Ernie.

"Why did you do that for that guy?" Stacy asked as she brought him some coffee.

"Stacy, if you could only have heard him perform. The mannerisms and the polish he has. It can't be wasted on a place like that. He gave me a CD of his work, we can play it later."

"You know, from what I saw of him he wasn't bad looking."

"Stacy, you've got enough problems without getting star struck."

"You never cease to amaze me Boss. Kennedy is already at the hospital. What do you say we go and see your girl?"

"I thought you'd never ask," Michael said, as they told the team goodnight and headed out the door.

Chapter 35

Paul Pratt and Brian Hunt had been on numerous waterfront stakeouts in Seattle. They asked to stake out pier 17. If something was going to happen they needed to know all about the area. About mid-morning Michael got a call from Johnnie Lima. They talked for several minutes. A boat was coming in Saturday night after midnight with drugs on board. Michael called Sommers and asked him to come over.

It was an hour before Sommers arrived and he didn't have the best of news.

"I'm being reassigned to San Diego tomorrow and I can't get out of it. I guess I will be reading about your exploits in the newspapers or on the local news."

"Damn it," Michael said handing Sommers some coffee. Is there anyone there we can work with?"

"Michael, you do have a way with words. Work is far from what I've had to endure since I've known you."

Michael smiled slightly and sipped his coffee.

"Well, there is Kohl. He and I are being flip-flopped in assignments but he's not the risk taker I am," Sommers said with a smile.

"Do you trust him to work like we did?"

"He goes strictly by the book. I don't think so."

They talked in general for a few minutes then they shook hands. Sommers again thanked him and said goodbye to the others. He left and Michael sat down to think.

The team had been busy and worked long hours to set up surveillance in key places. Scott couldn't wait until he could contribute. Besides sending the plane to Seattle to pick up some of the team, he loaded it down with some of their electronic gear. The last video camera was now about to be set up.

Chapter 36

Majestic Imports
San Leandro, California

Kennedy in full night gear looked over the entire car lot. His night vision mode showed no activity. He motioned to Jim Takata, who was spraying Freon against the fence to look for any laser monitors, that all was clear. Seeing none he cut a section in the fence at one of the stanchions. Both slipped through and made it to the rear door of Cattalo's home office. Jim scanned for any electronic locking devices then picked the lock. Kennedy looked the entire office over then pointed to the ceiling. Jim stood on a kitchen chair and removed the overhead air conditioning vent cover. Sliding the ninety-degree vent elbow off, he handed it to Kennedy. Opening the small bag he brought with him he removed a Co2 styled pellet gun and inserted a stainless steel shaft, eight inches long, in the barrel. Carefully aiming he fired the shaft into the roof above. It went about half way through. Jim cut the wires coming from the shaft to the length he needed then attached them to a small video camera. Securing the camera to the beam that ran across the ceiling and tapping into a hot line that ran along the beam, he called Arron on his cell phone. Arron had him adjust the direction to show the main table and bar area. They tested the audio feed and everything showed in place. Lastly he carefully replaced the vent. Putting the chair back in the kitchen he grabbed a towel from the sink. He wiped the chair off as well as the floor under the vent. They couldn't afford to have prints of their visit. They left the same way they came in and used some wire clips to reattach the cut fence as they had found it.

When they got back to the motel Arron showed them the results of their night's work. Michael let them go over a possible plan for intercepting the boat at pier 17. He had Stacy drive him over to the hospital.

"I've listened to that tape of Larry's and he is really good. Now I know why you helped him," Stacy commented.

"I called Glamour Tours today and talked with my old friend. I told him to consider handling him and let Larry go as far as he wanted. He said he would be waiting for Larry's call."

"Where will he go from there, I mean will he be singing in the city?"

"Actually, they put talent like Larry's out in places like the Indian Casinos in the mid-west to get them a lot of work. He's paid well and has an expense account. From there they can work up to the big shows. I know he will do all right."

As Michael walked by Wallace's office Jon motioned for him to come in.

"I just thought you'd like to know the pressure is decreasing at a very slow rate. I don't think we can get our hopes up just yet."

"That's very good news Jon. Will this keep happening?"

"I don't think it will fast enough but one never knows in conditions like these. I gave her a full exam today and she is experiencing some feeling in her upper pelvic area. It will take something short of spectacular to bring her legs back on line, so to speak."

"Thank you for keeping me informed. We still have time," Michael said as he stood up.

"Michael, that's the worst part of all this. She is now beyond the time frame of someone in her condition. Please don't build her up too far. She might not be able to withstand the fall, you either."

Michael stopped by the nurse's desk but there were no flowers. He smiled then walked to her room. She greeted him with open arms, arms that were getting stronger by the day.

"Where's my flower?"

"Close your eyes," he said then kissed her softly.

She smiled then asked him again.

"I just gave it to you, tulips."

She looked at him for a moment then started laughing. "Two lips, I get it. You're a funny guy."

They brought them dinner and as usual they shared.

Michael told her about Scott coming down to help and about what they had been doing.

"I know it won't be long before you have to give the word. I only wish I was there with you."

"I'll probably get shot in the butt while thinking of you. Then I can get a bed right next to yours."

She laughed and pinched his arm. "You know how we do this. Once it starts I will go all out to end it in the manner we know how to do best. I have made arrangements to cover all contingencies."

"No Michael, don't talk like that. You just do what you have to and come back. Ok?"

"You can count on it. We have to get to the islands and do some skinny-dipping, right?"

"We could start right now and practice," she said as she took his hand, brought it up under the blanket and placed it on her right breast.

He looked quickly over his shoulder to the hall. Nobody was there except Mason who had his back to them.

"You are so modest. I love that about you," she said as she squeezed his hand into her like the first night. "The nurse won't be in for a while yet."

He slowly pulled his hand back.

"How am I going to look walking out of here with my hat hanging from my lap?"

She burst out laughing at the thought. He stood up and straightened himself up.

"I'm sorry my darling, I just wanted to feel you touching me."

"We'll have plenty of time for that so do what you do and make your mind behave," he said sitting, then sat back down on the bed.

"When are you going to start the operation or is it too soon to know?"

"If everything goes as planned we should have a go inside two days," Michael answered.

"I know you will be careful. Just come back as soon as you can, promise?"

He promised then held her for a couple of minutes until the nurses came in. As he stood up to leave she said, "Hey, don't forget your hat."

She saw him start to look down then his face got flushed. He smiled, pointed his finger at her and then winked. She returned the gesture.

Chapter 37

The next morning Tamara ate bits and pieces of her breakfast and Michael just had coffee. She could see the worry on his face thought he tried to hide it.

"I had a long talk with Stacy last night. I wish I had what you two do, that unswerving trust that I can do no wrong. I don't have all the answers and that bothers me deeply," Michael said.

"We all do my darling. That makes you who you are. You have no idea how much you mean to both of us. When you walk out of here today I want you to clear your mind of me and everything that's happened regarding me…"

She put her fingers on his lips as he was about to stop her.

"I know you have to do what you think is right so you must stop letting me cloud your mind. I'm not going anywhere until you come back, whether that be tomorrow or two days from now. You will come back, I know it, I feel it."

He held her tightly for a few minutes. She realized all the ramifications he was facing and she tried to assure him she was fine with it. He could sense her fears and her looking ahead with all the positive thoughts she had.

"Hey, today I start my water therapy. Doctor Wallace says it will be good for me. Want to come into the tub with me?"

He smiled as he looked into her eyes. "There you go again. Is that all you ever think about?"

"Yes, and you better get used to it. Now get out of here and go play."

The nurses came in and she watched him walk out. She asked God to keep them all safe and to bring him back to her.

* *

He arrived back at the lodge to find R.C. had arrived along with the rest of the team. The lodge had a meeting room behind the office and they all assembled there. They listened to Brian and Paul as they laid out what they found out in their surveillance of pier 17. They had acquired copies of the blue prints of all the warehouses from the hall of records. They were spread out across the wall. After several hours of discussions, R.C. suggested several men come from the waterside of the pier to seal off the only escape route yet unguarded. The suggestion was adopted. One suggestion that didn't sit well with Michael at first was for him to control the operation from a distance. Playing the role of backup wasn't his style, but reluctantly agreed to it. His team would be fully armed and ready just in case. There had been no word from those watching the camera installed at Cattalo's office. Sarino was still nowhere to be found. Michael knew he would surface eventually and then Sarino would be his.

Chapter 38

C.J. was the only team member not to come down because he had the flu. It was R.C.'s decision to leave him there, as he was one-step short of being hospitalized. Michael talked with Marsha back at the plant and things were going as planned. Carl was having no problems as production and sales were holding steady. He told Carl he would be unavailable for a few days. Brian told Michael he was needed in the clubhouse. When they arrived several of the team was huddled around the monitor Arron had set up.

"There's Cattalo and that ones Sal Danza," Arron pointed out then turned the sound volume up.

Cattalo was having a final meeting with his men regarding the shipment coming in. The time was set for one o'clock in the morning. Cattalo ranted on about how the last shipment was bungled saying he would be there to make sure nothing went wrong. When he finished his meeting they watched as the men left. Cattalo made himself a drink then moved the bar stool away from the end of the bar. He retrieved two large shopping bags from the table then tilted a small decorative statue on the back counter. The bar separated in the middle and slid open about four feet. Below the bar was a three by three foot by one foot rectangle shaped safe. Cattalo took stacks of cash from the shopping bags and carefully placed them in the void. He stood up and tilted the statue again causing the bar to return to its original position.

"I've got to get me a statue like that," Michael laughed as Stacy poured him some more coffee.

Michael sat down with R.C., Scott, Brian, Jim, and Kennedy to go over the final plan. It bothered Michael that Cattalo had no mention of Tony Sarino.

* * * * * * * * * * * * * * * * * * * *

At midnight the team had taken their pre-determined positions. They could see men going in and out of the warehouse that took up half the pier. Michael and his team watched from the second story balcony of the closest warehouse on the wharf before the pier jettisoned out. Their night vision glasses worked well to cut through the unlit areas.

"Everything looks normal," Michael said in his mouthpiece. "Now we wait."

Stacy looked at her watch. "It's twelve thirty-five."

A minute later Arron said there were cars coming. They watched as three cars came down the wharf then on to pier 17. Stopping at the warehouse the vehicles' occupants got out and went in, leaving one man outside.

"It's too quiet Scott," Michael said as he continued to look around. "Even with the noise below us it's too quiet."

"I know what you mean."

They watched as a large fishing boat came down the bay and headed in.

"Team leader, it's not getting any warmer in this water, I hope they get tied up soon."

"R.C. you've got enough scotch in you to keep you warm. You don't even need a wet suit," Michael said as he watched the boat nearing the pier.

Michael continued to scan the area. He just felt something wasn't right. There were several cargo storage vaults on both the dock and pier which would give the team cover if they needed it.

"To all teams, take Cattalo alive if possible. R.C., sink the boat if they try to leave."

All teams answered.

Michael watched as the first crate touched the pier from the boat, then Michael said "Go."

As he looked down at the teams converging he saw something move just below him to his left. He picked up the larger night scope. He looked again. He saw Johnnie Lima in plain clothes with a badge hanging from his neck on a chain.

"It's a trap, abort and get out of there," Michael yelled.

It was too late. Several of the cargo storage vault doors crashed open. DEA and ATF S.W.A.T. teams poured onto the pier and wharf, surrounding the entire ground team. Michael grabbed Stacy and pulled her into the darkened warehouse just as they heard, "DEA, drop your weapon and stand up."

Scott did as they ordered and they were on him quickly. Michael and Stacy ducked down behind some large crates as several of the officer's luminated the warehouse with their flashlights. They moved Scott along the catwalk and to the stairs leading down to the wharf. There was a lot of activity at the boat site and a few shots were fired. They could see the boat leaving at high speed back into the channel. Michael had just taken Stacy's arm to head out when they heard a loud explosion. Through the dirty windows of the warehouse they could see a giant ball of flames erupting from the boat's location. Several smaller explosions followed as Stacy followed Michael across the warehouse. They carefully made it down to the lower floor as everyone there had gone out to see the burning boat.

Once outside they stayed close to the building. They dove to the ground as two large step vans drove by them and stopped about thirty feet away. The door behind them said Men. They heard a lot of voices coming so they backed into the room.

"Damn it smells in here, doesn't anybody clean this place," Stacy said putting her hand over her nose.

Michael rubbed a small spot through the dirty window by the door. He saw they were loading the Rangers into the closest van. He also saw Agent Kohl talking with Johnnie Lima who wore an ATF jacket.

"I have to take a leak, hold on a second," they heard.

"Yeah, me too," another voice said.

Michael grabbed Stacy and pulled her into one of the stalls without a door. There was hardly enough room for one person let alone two. The lights went on and they heard two people come in. They listened to the sound of zippers go down.

"This is one sweet bust. I can't believe they gave up so quick…"

His sentence ended as Michael's 9mm caught him above the ear. The second one fell just as hard. Stacy helped Michael remove their jackets and hats. Slipping them on, Michael looked back out of the spot in the window. The other truck was pulling away and there were a few ATF men walking towards pier 17.

"Come on guys, what's taking you so long?" The door opened and another man looked in.

Michael grabbed him by his collar and pulled him. Stacy laid him out cold with the butt of her automatic.

They shut the light off and then walked out. Michael went around to the right side of the truck and got in. Stacy started the truck, turned around, and started away from the wharf. They could see the other truck stopped ahead at a light so she slowed down. They closed within a half block of the other truck as the light changed. They had given the other truck almost a one-block lead and watched as it turned right on a yellow light. They sat there at the red light. Michael saw a sign ahead showing the freeway south and told Stacy to take it. She headed straight and onto the freeway. Surprisingly nobody was following them. It took them ten minutes to the Millbrae exit.

"I can't wait to see the look on their faces when we open the doors," Michael said quietly.

Stacy drove to the lodge and parked on the backside out of sight of the road. They went to the rear of the truck and sprung open the gate. The look on the faces of everyone inside was a picture in itself. Laughter broke out as Michael stood there with his arms crossed.

"I swear Boss, you are something," Scott said as they helped him out.

"Keep it down," Michael said as he cut the plastic tie around Scott's wrist then gave him the knife. Kennedy and Mason went and opened the truck's side arms locker. They retrieved their gear.

Chad got in the van and followed Stacy and Michael in the Escalade. They had to hide the van as far away as they could.

They started across the Dumbarton Bridge.

"Stacy, I want to thank you for being there for Tamara, it means a lot to both of us."

"She and I are so close, like you two are. We confide in each other."

Michael lit two cigarettes and handed one to her.

Stacy turned off the bridge onto state road 4 that headed to Fremont. Within a mile he told her to pull into an industrial park. Chad drove the police van in between a row of semi trailers then wiped the cabs interior down quickly.

Once back at the lodge, Michael learned Cattalo and a few of his men eluded capture. They had been watching the monitor of his office and he hadn't returned yet. R.C. told Michael they almost keeled over seeing everyone waiting when they got back. Michael left the clubhouse and went back to his room. He took a long hot shower to clear his head.

Chapter 39

Federal courthouse
San Francisco, California

Everyone outside the closed room could hear the shouting by the police commissioner.

"I can't believe all the money and man hours you've spent on this operation and it all went up in smoke. We have three men in the hospital with concussions and we lost a truckload of prisoners. Have I left anything out? The Mayor has been on my ass for two hours. Would anyone here like to call him and explain all this? No, I didn't think so. And another thing Agent Kohl, where were your men at the time the trucks drove away?"

Nobody said a word, especially Kohl. The butt chewing lasted another fifteen minutes then the commissioner left in disgust.

When it was over, Kohl called Sommers and told him what went down. Sommers had no words of advice for him before he hung up. Sommers just shook his head and began to laugh.

Michael called and talked briefly to Tamara. She was glad everything worked out for the team. He told her he would be up to see her for breakfast.

* * * * * * * * * * * * * * * * * * * *

Around five Jim came for Michael. Half the team stood watching the monitor. They listened to Cattalo yell about the night's happenings. He went as far as knocking a dozen or more glasses on the back shelf down to the floor.

"He's really pissed," Arron offered.

"I guess so. He lost half his men and the entire shipment," Michael said with a slight smile.

"And where the hell have you been?" Cattalo yelled at someone who had just walked in.

"Sarino," Michael said.

They continued to listen but their talk of what was next on their agenda was vague. About five minutes later Cattalo said something that got Michael's attention.

"I'm staying right here tonight. You do what you're supposed to do and we can still come out of this with something."

"Do we have anybody at the dealership or close by?" Michael asked.

The answer was negative.

"Assemble a team R.C. We need Cattalo. Maybe with him we can force Sarino to come to us."

R.C. picked six men and they discussed a plan.

"I'm getting hungry, how about some dinner?" Stacy asked Michael.

"Sure, why not."

When they got back R.C. and the team had already gone. The rain had just begun. Kennedy had just left for the hospital to relieve Chad a little early. Michael smiled at his dedication.

"Is Cattalo still there?" Michael asked Arron.

"Sure is. He's cooled off some."

"What time does R.C. plan to hit him?"

"In about an hour. Want me to come get you when it starts, Boss?"

"No, let R.C. have his day, I'm a little tired. I might stretch out for a few hours," Michael said, then left.

He didn't even turn on a light when he entered his room. His shoulders and neck were stiff and sore. Maybe I'm getting too old for this line of work, he thought as he turned on the shower.

Chapter 40

R.C. and Scott sat in the car on the side street adjacent to Majestic Motors. The rain came down harder as they watched a third car arrive and two men get out. Within minutes the lights to the dealership went out leaving on only the corner lights of the lot and front sign luminated.

"How you guys holding up?" R.C. asked.

"All I know it's damn wet out here," Jim said from their position under one of the building's overhangs.

"Brian, how you doing?"

"Hell, it doesn't rain this much in Seattle. We're in the detailing lean-to. Just give us the word."

The three employees from the dealership ran to their cars parked on the back lot.

"Talk to me base, what's happening?" R.C. said.

"Several are getting ready to come out. The rest are just sitting and talking," Arron said.

"We see them. We'll take it from here," R.C. said.

Three men in the car headed for the gate. When they were within twenty feet of the gate the car stopped suddenly. The driver put it into reverse and sped back toward the house.

"We've been spotted. Let's take 'em down," R.C. said as he and Scott got out of their car.

As they ran across the side street, one of the three in the car fired at them. The lights in the house shut off. The car stopped and all three got out, using the doors as shields. They fired a number of rounds at R.C.'s position before Jim took out the driver with three shots. The other two fired in Jim's direction but only shattered the windows of several cars around him. Mason appeared about thirty feet from one of the men who had now turned in his direction and froze from his appearance. Mason fired a two-second volley from his pulse cannon. Glass shattered, the trunk lid blew open, and the shooter took four rounds through his body. The guy on the passenger side tried to make it to the front door of the house. He was cut down by Paul who was roughly twenty feet from him. The back door of the house opened and another one of Cattalo's men came out shooting. Brian put four rounds into him as he fell near the fence. Paul climbed the fence and stayed low along the house to the back door. He reached for the handle as Brian took aim with his .45. Paul turned the handle to open the door and the door flew open with automatic rifle rounds flying out. Brian emptied his clip through the opening but hit nobody. Paul took a step out from the side of the house. Just as he fired his 9mm someone from the window above fired twice. Paul took one round through his right collarbone and into his upper back. He fell back into the fence then to the ground.

"Mason get over here," Brian yelled in his mouthpiece. "Paul's down."

Scott and R.C. had reached the front door of the house and they started taking fire from inside. Mason came around the back corner of the house.

"They're all around the door," Brian said, pointing in that direction.

As the thunder rumbled loudly, Mason laid a three second burst along the backside of the house and door. Windows shattered and the door shut then reopened as the bullets went into it. One body came out head first into the muddy asphalt and a second one didn't make it quite that far. The lightning flashed brightly again luminating the entire lot. Over the thunder that followed Mason laid another three second burst along the rest of the windows on that side.

"Cattalo, come out and you won't be harmed," R.C. yelled.

Another volley of automatic weapons fire rained down on their position.

"I think that means no," Scott said wiping some mud off his forehead.

"You think?" R.C. said comically as he threw a concussion grenade through the front window. The windows across the entire front and far side of the house blew out which sent everyone ducking for cover. The lightning flashed and the thunder followed seconds later. Jim followed Mason in the rear door as Scott and Brian went in the front. Jim flipped the hall light on then went back outside to help Paul. Three were dead in the rear of the house. Five more were down in the living room.

"Cattalo should have come out when he had the chance," R.C. said as he looked at him leaning against the sofa. "Make a quick search of the place then let's get out of here."

Scott and Brian took Paul to the hospital.

Chapter 41

Knob Hill
Connerly estate

"I'm going up to Sacramento today but I'll be back sometime Sunday. I want you here when I get back," Matthias said as he handed a suit to the houseman.

"I'll be here, like always," Samantha answered.

"It's funny, you always go visit your sweet sister every time I leave town but she never visits here. Don't you find that a little unusual?"

"No, I don't. You go out of your way to start an argument with her then she goes away very upset. Why do you do that? Is it to hurt me?"

"She can stay away from here for good and I wouldn't mind. She's always trying to get you to protest for her group's causes, yeah, causes that make my job harder. Why doesn't she just find herself another husband? How many has she had now, three, four, or have I lost count?"

"I'll be downstairs. I would rather not listen to you continually downgrade Victoria. She's been nothing but gracious to you."

He met her at the bedroom door and grabbed her arm.

"You're hurting me, please…"

"You're both getting to where you've outlived your usefulness. One of these days I'll be rid of both of you. Get out of my sight," Matthias said as he shoved her into the hallway.

The houseman carried his luggage out of the room as Matthias went into the bathroom. Removing a syringe from a drawer he inserted the needle into a small insulin bottle and then laid it down on the sink. He rolled up his sleeve and administered the dosage. His medicine kit was packed away so he threw the syringe into the wastebasket.

The chauffer took his luggage out as he neared the front door. “Just be here when I get back,” Matthias said as he slammed the front door.

Samantha stood at the front windows and watched his car disappear down the long drive. She rubbed her arm where he had grabbed her. “I’ll outlive you.”

Chapter 42

The traffic was heavy as Michael and Stacy drove south on Interstate 280. She took the Millbrae Exit and headed east. Brian Hunt had located a motor lodge that received very little business since the freeway was finished. Michael bought all twenty rooms for three days which delighted the retired owners. They had never put the No Vacancy sign on since they bought the lodge twenty years earlier. The lodge sat back off the road about a hundred fifty feet. The tall trees along the road gave them plenty of privacy.

"We want to thank you Mr. Canon. Harry and I have decided that since you've rented all our rooms, that he and I would drive down the coast to Monterey for a couple of days and surprise our grandkids," Mrs. Cooperton said. "The house cleaning ladies will be by each morning at eight. It shouldn't take them but an hour or so to clean up. I don't think the lodge could be in better hands than with the federal bureau."

"Do they call you mister at the bureau?" Harry asked.

Michael smiled. "No sir, it's actually Special Agent. I like to drop all that when we get away from the red tape and bureaucracy."

"I don't blame you at all," Harry said. "Are you a Special Agent too?"

"No sir, I'm just Agent Brock Mason. He's the boss."

"We are looking forward to the convention over the weekend but we like to sleep where it's nice and quiet," Michael added. "In town you can't even have a quiet dinner for all the loud music of today."

"Isn't that the truth? That's why we bought land way out here. We saw it coming years ago," Harry said as he handed Michael four more room keys.

"Here is a number where we can be reached in case of an emergency," Mrs. Cooperton said. "We'll see you on Monday. Have a good time at the convention."

"Have a safe trip ma'am, sir," Brock said, shaking Harry's hand.

Michael and Mason headed back to their room.

"You know Harry, those men being here has renewed my faith in the government. Did you hear that ma'am and sir? I haven't heard that in years."

"I did Mama. I know one thing, with them around there won't be any trouble. Come on, let's go pack and head out now."

* * * * * * * * * * * * * * * * * * * *

Brock started laughing when he got back to his room with some of the team.

"I swear Boss, you could charm a fur coat off a mink."

Michael smiled as Stacy brought him some coffee.

"I told them we were in for the federal law enforcement meetings in town. They assumed we were from the FBI so I went along with it."

"The scary part is I'm starting to think just like you Boss. But how come you got to be a Special Agent and me only an agent?" Brock asked.

"If you want to pay the bill for this whole place, you can be the Special."

They all had a good laugh.

Everyone left soon after but Michael who asked Stacy to stay. Michael stacked a couple of pillows up behind him as he sat back on the bed.

"I called R.C. and told him I want everybody down with all the gear. I don't know what's going to happen but it's best we have the entire force behind us," Michael said as he set his coffee on his nightstand.

"I think I feel better knowing we have numbers too," she said sitting by his feet and bringing her legs under her.

"What would you be doing if you were home right now?"

"That's easy, getting my trucks ready for the weekend's race. Wait a minute, you're not sending me away, are you?"

Michael sipped some coffee. "What, and have to drink Mason's coffee?"

She smiled at the thought and slapped his hip.

"Like before, I want you with me, Jim and Kennedy too."

"I can live with that Boss."

"I asked you to stay because I have something to ask of you. I don't know how this might turn out, hell we never do. I would ask you to be close to Tamara if I should go down."

She put her coffee on the nightstand and sat next to him. Her face was full of concern at what he said.

"She's going to need help at least when she's released."

"Michael, please don't talk like that. We're going to come through this all right. The three of us are a team. We'll never be broken up. I promise to be with her as long as she needs me. We'll all get through this."

"Hey, you know it's after midnight? You need to get some rest."

She got up and put their coffee cups in the bathroom. He worried about her getting hurt or worse, killed. She gave him a hug then went to the door. "Night Boss."

Chapter 43

The rain was falling harder now as a car wound around the last curve and then stopped below the mansion. Its occupant got out carrying a small satchel and proceeded to the stone gate at the wall in front of him. The cold rain struck him hard in the back as he used a hydraulic cutter on the heavy chain securing the gate. He looked up at the big mansion above him. The heavy rain had forced the night guard to move to the other side of the balcony. Thirty feet more brought him to the steel door of the wine cellar. Again he had to cut the chain, as the door hadn't been used in years. He pushed it open then closed it behind him. He used his flashlight to light the narrow passageway. Gravel that lined his way up to the wine cellar door now crunched under his weight. Pushing the door inward found him staring at rows of vintage wines from years past. He followed the worn out board floor to the door at the end of the damp and musty smelling room. He pushed on the door and it opened slightly. He slipped his wet raincoat off and laid it on a bench next to him. Slipping out of his shoe totes, he entered the next room. He was met by DeSeno holding a large towel.

"You're late," DeSeno said.

"If you've done your job then there's nothing to worry about. Let's go," the man snapped.

Vencenti's bedroom was on the opposite side of the second floor from the other six bedrooms.

"Did you mix the sedative into their drinks?"

"Yes."

DeSeno left him and went downstairs to the parlor. He poured two drinks. He gave one to the guard sitting in the living room, his back to the upper balcony.

"What a rotten night to be out."

Just then they saw a flash of lightning and a few seconds later a roll of thunder rumbled.

The intruder saw the guard's back then walked quietly to Vencenti's bedroom door and went in.

"I'll drink to that," the guard said.

The intruder stood next to the armoire and looked at the two sleeping. The light from the window gave him all the help he needed as he slowly moved next to Samantha. She lay on her back with her head turned slightly towards Angelo. Her right arm lay along her side on top of the quilt. The man stared at her peaceful demeanor for a moment and then pulled a syringe from his shirt pocket. He looked at Angelo and smiled. Putting his left hand on her arm just above her elbow, he placed the small half-inch long needle to her skin then pushed slightly. The sedative had her in a deep sleep to where she felt no pain as he depressed the plunger. He stood up and walked back to the armoire. Samantha's body made a small violent movement which startled the man for a moment. The man looked at Angelo who just kept snoring. The intruder slowly opened the door and saw the guard was still talking to DeSeno. He left the same way he came in.

Chapter 44

The sun hadn't come up yet as a knock at the door woke Angelo up. A maid entered the room and set a tray containing coffee, two cups, and a rose on his nightstand. He thanked her and she left. He sat up and poured a little coffee in both cups.

"How about some coffee to begin your morning, Samantha?"

Getting no answer he looked over at her. She lay motionless. He stood up and walked around the bed. The first thing he saw was the syringe stuck in her arm. He cried out, fell to his knees and put his arms on her. The door opened.

"Is everything all right, Angelo"

"Get Dominic for me."

Within a minute Dominic entered the room and Angelo told him to shut the door. Angelo was sitting next to Samantha, his head in his hands.

"This is not good Angie, we need to do something," Dominic said as he looked at the syringe.

"Who would do such a thing?"

"Angie, please, let me take care of this. I'll take her to her home while there's still time."

"Yes, do what you must but treat her with respect. Here, take her bracelet. The house security code is inside the band."

Dominic called for two of his men. He told one of them to keep everyone on the north side of the house. As Angelo went into the bathroom and closed the door, Dominic wrapped Samantha in the top quilt on the bed. His man returned. They carried her downstairs and out the east patio doors where two more men waited.

It was an hour before Dominic returned. One of the men gave him a dry towel as he slid out of his wet shoes.

"Where's Angelo?"

"He's in the den by the fireplace. He hasn't moved since you left."

Dominic poured two brandies then entered the parlor.

"Here, drink this Angelo."

Angelo looked up at him then took the drink. "Is she sleeping peacefully?"

"Yes, we laid her in her own bed."

"Who would do such a thing? She never hurt anyone."

"Angelo, please listen to me for a moment. I think it was Matthias Connerly who ordered this. He left town when she came here. He knows this is the only way he can get to you."

"I touched the needle; it has my prints on it."

"I took care of that. Here, see?"

Angelo looked at the barrel of a syringe in Dominic's hand.

"Connerly is a diabetic. I carefully replaced this part with one he had thrown in the trashcan in the bathroom. They can never trace this back to you, never."

"Thank you my friend. I owe you my life," Angelo said.

"Our friendship has always been enough for me," Dominic said as he threw the syringe barrel in the fireplace.

"Excuse me sir, there is a police lieutenant here to see you."

Dominic gave Angelo his arm as they walked to the front door.

"Angelo Vencenti, I have a warrant to search the premises. I'm Detective Harper, and you are duly served. These men are witnesses to the fact. Please ask your men to stand down."

"Alfredo, call my attorney and have him come over."

As the six officers searched the house Angelo sat in the parlor and looked the warrant over, then handed it to Dominic.

"It was Connerly. He signed it before he left two hours ago."

It was twenty minutes before Detective Harper came into the parlor.

"Mr. Vencenti, I would like to ask you several questions if I may."

Angelo nodded his head.

"Do you know a Samantha Connerly?"

"Yes I do. Her husband and I go back a long way. Why do you ask?"

"When was the last time you talked to her?"

"Why only this morning she called and asked me to talk to Matthias. I guess they were arguing. He grabbed the phone from her and gave me an earful. Why, what has happened?"

"Nothing Mr. Vencenti, thank you for allowing us to come in."

Dominic followed the Detective to the door then watched them drive away.

"Angelo, I am going to look into this. Someone here either in the house did this or helped someone from the outside. You might be next."

"Thank you Dominic. Bring this person to me once you find them."

"You handled the police very well," Dominic said, handing Angelo another small brandy.

"You know, that happened just like I said over twenty years ago and I never forgot that. It just came out like it was yesterday."

Chapter 45

Michael kept his promise and had breakfast with Tamara.

"You are getting stronger. I think I need to start exercising again just to keep up with you," Michael declared.

"I feel that I am too. Doctor Wallace says I'm overdoing it. I just don't want to be a weakling when I get out of here. How's your neck, still bothering you?"

"Not right now. I stood under a hotter than usual shower, that seemed to do the trick."

"I hear you had a visitor yesterday. You don't have to tell me if you don't want to."

"I had doctor Wallace recommended an attorney. I'm having a living will drawn up. If anything happens to me I've left everything I have to you."

Michael was taken by her words. He kissed her.

"Actually, I have done something similar for you. I never want you to be in need of anything again."

They finished their now cold breakfast and she told him to get going so she could go to therapy. They kissed and he left as Catherine came in.

Michael's cell phone rang as Stacy drove them from the hospital in the Lincoln. He talked for several minutes then hung up.

"I need to go back to the city. They need for me to sign legal documents and papers for the company. It's set up for three tomorrow afternoon."

He had Stacy drive him to the plane.

Molly brought him some hot tea then they all sat down while he waited for a reply to a fax. Michael started getting flashbacks of everything that had happened thus far. He pulled his cell phone out and went into the memory. He viewed the number then sent it.

"I'd like to speak to Mr. Vencenti."

"Your name."

"Michael Canon."

It was quiet in the plane as he waited about a minute.

"Michael. Thank you for calling. How can I help you?"

"I just thought you might be interested in knowing Frank Cattalo won't be bothering you anymore."

"I must say you have been busy since we last talked," Angelo stated.

"I am asking you for your help again. I want Tony Sarino."

"Ah, Mr. Canon, ask me to give you anything but that."

"Let me sweeten the offer. My sources have told me that within the last few weeks someone has come into your organization or maybe into your home for reasons of their own. I will give you the name if you give me your Godson."

Memories of the past hours went through Angelo's head as he pondered Michael's request.

"Michael, I can't do what you ask of me. I think all of this is leading to one thing. You and I will have a problem. I was praying it would not come down to this."

"I am flying out of here shortly. When I return I will call you first before I proceed," Michael said, then hung up.

"Are we taking on the big boy?" Ernie asked.

"I knew it would come down to this sooner or later. Everybody stay on your toes."

* *

Angelo sat quietly pondering Michael's words. Dominic came into the study. "Angie, we need to start getting ready for the wake. You said you wanted to be there by six."

"Dominic, my friend. I am faced with a decision I only had to make once before in my life."

He explained the entire story to Dominic who listened attentively.

"I think first things first," Dominic said. "I might suggest we send someone to, let's say, talk with this Canon before he leaves. After that we can deal with the other problem Canon said we had."

Angelo pondered the suggestion. "You do what you think is best Dominic. Make it clean."

Chapter 46

Ernie turned on the TV at the back of the plane for the weather report. They watched it for several minutes and then a "Special News" ticker came across the screen.

"This is John Savage at the Channel 11 news desk. We have just received word that a high-ranking official in San Francisco's political machine has been arrested. For more, we go out to San Francisco International with our own Sharron Cameron...Sharron?"

"Thank you John. Just moments ago, as you can see on the monitor, three California Department of Law Enforcement officers arresting Assistant State Attorney Matthias Connerly in connection with the death of his wife, Samantha Lyndon Connerly. As you know, she was found dead in her home early Saturday morning. Other law enforcement officials here on the scene have refused to expound on the next step in the investigation. For Channel 11 news, on the scene at San Francisco International Airport, this is Sharron Cameron."

"Well that just goes to show you crime doesn't pay," Ernie said as he turned the TV off.

The last fax had just come in when Michael's cell phone rang.

"Boss, one of the teams has picked up Tony Sarino's car heading out of downtown from the wharf. R.C. is trying to triangulate his exact location," Arron said.

"We're at the plane, who is closest to us?"

"Steve and Mason are heading your way right now."

Michael hung up and told them what was said. He went to the last overhead compartment, picked three 9mm clips from the box inside and put them in his coat pocket.

"Give me a couple too; I only have one with me," Stacy said, as she walked back to him.

Michael closed the overhead door. "You're not going."

He walked past her and she started to follow him then stopped. Walking back to the overhead compartment she grabbed several clips. By the time she came out of the plane the Escalade was pulling up next to the Lincoln. Scott got out of the SUV and started talking to Michael. Stacy jumped into the front seat.

"Stacy, I can't let you go," Michael said as he took off his coat by the side door.

"Scott, get your ass in the front seat. We're out of here." "I'm going Boss and that's that," Stacy said putting on her safety harness.

Scott looked at Michael who just nodded with his head to Scott.

Stacy flipped on the GPS tracker and told Scott to look up the number for metro San Francisco. He told her and she punched it in. She drove off the tarmac and onto the airport frontage road leading to the freeway. Mason helped Michael slip on his Kevlar turtleneck as Stacy weaved in and out of traffic. Scott monitored R.C.'s transmission through the earpiece.

"What's he saying Scott? Are we close?" Mason asked several times.

Stacy nudged Scott in the arm and he looked her way. "Open the glove box and get that adapter."

He did as he was told.

"Put that end in the cigar lighter and that end into the earpiece," Stacy said as she almost ran over a small car that had swerved into her lane. She turned the radio on. "What channels…look at the book?"

"109."

Scott turned the radio dial until they heard R.C. talking to Jim Takata.

Stacy opened the center console, pulled out a hand mike and handed it back to Michael.

"R.C., we're picking you up nice and clear."

"I've got ya. Keep heading in the direction you're going. Now, pull the lighter out one click and you should get the location of everybody."

Scott did so and two blips appeared on the GPS screen.

"We see them," Michael said.

Stacy turned off of 101 and onto Market. She glanced down at the monitor as she drove.

"Their signal's getting stronger," they heard Brian say. "Hell, we have to be right on top of…shit, they're right in front of us."

"Jimmy, turn around and come back up O'Farrell," R.C. said.

"They're driving a new Lexus, color white, three men inside," Brian said as he gave pursuit.

Michael and the others watched as their green dots started coming together. The closer they got to the center grid is where the traffic got heavier and the intersection stoplights were not working to their advantage. Stacy jumped several red lights but it still wasn't enough to close in as the other two blips were now going away from them.

Chapter 47

Angelo Vencenti's car phone rang. Dominic answered it then handed it to Angelo saying it was Tony.

"Yes Anthony, what is it?"

"I think that guy you talked about has found me. At least his men have," Sarino yelled.

"Calm down, are you sure it's them and not the police?"

"No it's not the police. I've never seen these guys before and they're still chasing us."

"Where are you at? Are you close to the house?" Angelo asked.

"No. I'm down by Union square. Can you help me or not?"

"Tony, I can't help you right now. I'm going someplace. You just go…"

"I don't think you're listening to me. They hit Frank last night and now they're on me. I need your help."

"Listen to me, try and get away from them. Go to the house if you can get there. I'll call and tell them you're coming. Do this!" Angelo yelled then handed the phone to Dominic.

Dominic called and informed them of Tony's peril.

"If Canon's men can find Tony then we have a big problem. Who did you send for Canon?"

"Petra and Vasselaro."

"They're good boys. When they're done all of this will stop," Angelo said as they neared the funeral home.

* * * * * * * * * * * * * * * * * * * *

World Airways Jetport
Challenger 6

Vasselaro drove slowly down the concourse and approached the private plane area. They scanned the planes then Petra spotted Michael's Lincoln next to the Challenger 6.

"I don't see anyone around. He must be on the plane. Pull up next to his car," Petra said as he put a silencer on his 9mm.

Ernie and Molly were working on the heating elements for the coffee urn. It sometimes came on when they didn't want it to and vice versa. Ernie had solved the problem. As he was putting on the last wire nut they heard a car door shut. He wiped his hands off and walked to the plane's door. Petra approached and asked for a Mr. Canon.

"He's not available. I'm his pilot, can I help you?"

"Petra raised his arm, fired his silenced automatic, and hit Ernie in the right shoulder just under the collarbone. The force knocked him back into the galley and onto the floor. Petra rushed on board and stopped Molly from calling on her cell.

"Put it down and sit here."

She did as he said. Vasselaro came aboard and began to search the plane. He soon returned saying nobody else was with them.

"We'll wait. Get the car out of sight."

Before he could take a step towards the door they heard a voice.

"Say moose and squirrel."

As their eyes looked down to the floor Ernie fired off four rounds from his 9mm. Petra took one round through his upper chest and throat. Vasselaro fell from one in his stomach and eye. Molly screamed as she jumped up to get away from Petra who had nearly fallen on her. She went to the door and looked out. Seeing nobody else outside she came to Ernie's side. She grabbed a galley towel and shoved it against his shoulder. He held his hand on it and told her to call R.C. He was anguished in pain and then began laughing to himself.

"I always wanted to say that."

Brandon and Dawson had just left the lodge and were approaching the main airport. They got R.C.'s call and were the first to arrive. They secured the area by the time the paramedics arrived.

Chapter 48

Union Square
San Francisco

"Where's he at Richard? Are they heading back in our direction?" Michael asked.

"He's hard to follow, keeps turning left and right then comes back your way. Stop where you are, hopefully they'll come right by you."

Stacy pulled over at the corner and they waited. She tapped her fingers on the steering wheel as she looked around. Michael lit two cigarettes and gave her one. She thanked him then rolled her window down.

"Michael, someone tried a hit at the plane," R.C. said. "Ernie is down but he'll live. He's on the way to the hospital. I think they were looking for you."

"Call Doctor Wallace and tell him Ernie's coming in. Let's hope he's still there."

"We lost his signal or he's not talking," Brian said.

"We're dead too or out of range," Jim said.

Just then they saw the white Lexus and it was flying low. It hit the intersection and momentarily went airborne. Two cars that Sarino went between spun out and hit other cars. Stacy hit the throttle and quickly made her way into the intersection and smoked the tires making a u-turn amidst all the cars. She was doing seventy by the time she had gone the first block weaving in and out through the traffic.

"There he is," Scott said pointing ahead.

"He's heading for the interstate bypass, don't lose him," Michael said.

"Ah hell, look behind us," Mason said.

An unmarked police car with two men inside was right on them. A red light flashed on the dash and blue lights flashed back and forth across the grill.

"Pull over Stacy," Michael said.

"But we'll..."

"Just do it."

She did as Michael ordered but applied the brake slowly at the same time flipping the switch on the dash for the air bag control.

"We have too much armament to get out of this one," Scott said.

"Just hang on everybody, I'm gonna try something," Stacy said as her speedometer read forty-five, forty, then thirty-five. Are they right on us?"

"Stacy, just pull over," Michael said again.

"I've got it Boss, just hang onto something," Stacy ordered. "Where are they now?"

"Bumper to bumper about thirty feet back," Mason answered.

Fifteen, ten, and five, then she slammed on the brakes and put the Escalade in reverse. She rammed the police car and activated the front airbags inside the car. Dropping the Escalade in gear she smoked rubber for thirty feet and hit the bypass entrance.

"It'll take them at lease thirty seconds to get away from the bags," Stacy said, as she hit the interstate. "How about another cigarette, I seem to have lost mine."

Everybody laughed, then praised her for her antics. Scott gave her five and she reciprocated.

Michael lit two cigarettes and gave her one.

"Where did you learn that trick Stacy?" Scott asked.

"I used to be a cop. I know all the tricks. That one I had never tried but it seemed like the right time to see if it would work."

"Michael, are you still with us?"

"Yeah Richard, what's up?" he said pointing his finger at Stacy and grinning.

"The last transmission Brian got was Sarino talking to somebody about protecting him. He was upset that the person wasn't going to be someplace, or something like that. Got any ideas?"

"I don't think, I know. He was talking to Vencenti. We have to get off the streets. Have everybody meet back at the lodge."

Chapter 49

Angelo Vencenti's driver stopped in front of the Roseville Memorial Chapel. He opened the rear door of the limousine and helped Angelo out. Angelo, Dominic, and one of his men climbed the short stairs to the entrance. They were met by two men wearing carnations.

"I am Angelo Vencenti and I have come to pay my respects to Samantha Connerly."

"Wait here for one moment please."

They watched as the young man walked the length of the aisle and spoke to someone seated. In a moment he returned and showed them in.

"Hello Angelo. Thank you for coming. I am Samantha's sister Victoria. She spoke warmly of you."

"I am heartbroken we have to meet under these circumstances. I am truly sorry. My sympathy is with you."

He kissed her hand then turned towards the casket ahead of him. There were only three other people in the room which saddened Angelo. The three walked slowly to the front of the chapel. Dominic and his bodyguard said a short prayer then moved to one side. Angelo felt very weak and helpless as he looked at Samantha lying so still in front of him. He laid the rose on her crossed hands. He began to weep as he put his own hands on hers. He told her of his love for her as if she was only sleeping. In a few minutes he kissed his finger and touched her lips. He wiped his teary eyes then started towards Victoria. He asked her if he could sit with her for a minute.

"Samantha talked of you often over the years, Angelo. She couldn't have had a better friend in life," she said as she placed her hand on his.

"My heart is full of our memories. She has taken them with her too."

"I know she has and in our hearts she will always be with us. Thank you for coming Angelo. This has meant so much to her and to me. I have to leave. Will you walk me out?"

She took his arm and walked slowly to the door. They stopped, looked back for a moment at Samantha's casket, and then walked down to the car. She gave him a hug then said goodnight.

Chapter 50

Michael called Vencenti's home and was told he was out. The team checked all their gear and waited as R.C. laid out what they knew of the mansion. Arron had searched the internet and found a section on old Victorian homes in San Francisco. There were five pictures of Vencenti's house before he purchased it. Knowing Sarino and two others were already there they could only speculate that there could be possibly up to a dozen more they would face. The order Michael had given, that Sarino was Michael's mark would stand, even if the opportunity to take him out existed. It was Michael's vendetta now and they all accepted it.

Brian and Chad had gone to the mansion and parked a half block away. Using a telescopic night vision scope they scanned the entire layout, moving quietly to different vantage points. They called back to R.C. giving him the momentary locations of guards at the mansion. The last thing Michael wanted was to have a war with Vencenti or any other family. He sat there and watched the team talk, killing time until they had to begin. He thought about Ernie and Paul already down. Nearly a dozen had given their lives for him over the past few years. How many more lives would be snuffed out tonight? A car drove up. It was Scott and he came in carrying a long package.

"Have any trouble?" Michael asked as Scott laid it on the table.

"No, I told them I was having trouble with cougars at the ranch and wanted to take care of them humanely."

"Tranquilizer guns. Is this what I think it's for?" Arron asked opening a box containing six darts.

"Arron, you and Kennedy will take out as many outside guards as you can. We're not there to wipe out everything that moves. We won't have a choice with all of them but we'll try and keep the casualties down to a minimum. It will also increase our rate of survival. I'm going in for Sarino then we're out of there. R.C., we need an escape plan, as no doubt the police will be on the house like flies when the shooting starts."

As the two shooters calibrated their rifles, R.C. and the others worked on the escape route. Michael walked outside and Stacy followed. He leaned against the building and lit two cigarettes. Stacy took one and stood next to him.

"I guess it won't do me any good to tell you to stay in the Escalade?" Michael asked.

"They don't do it in the movies, why should I?" she answered.

"I always hated that too. Stay in the car…ok…the next thing you see is the butcher knife wielding psychopath has her in the kitchen," Michael said, then laughed a little.

"It's no worse when the guy's buddy gets shot so the other idiot jumps up on the hood of the car and starts shooting in all directions. You know they're gonna blast his stupid ass," Stacy countered.

Michael flipped his cigarette. "You stay where I know you're safe, ok?"

"Ok Boss."

Chapter 51

The quarter moon didn't give them the light they would have liked. Brian would spot targets for Arron and Chad would for Kennedy. Michael and the rest of the team split up into three groups of two, then laid back to let the shooting team commence.

The four stayed low as they worked their way to a spot roughly one hundred fifty feet from the front gates of the mansion.

"There are two guards inside the gate," Brian said. "One is on each side of the drive on the grass."

"I'll take the one on the right," Arron said to Kennedy, as he lay on the grass and took aim. "On the count of three."

Just then headlights appeared from the street coming towards them. They kept their heads down as Vencenti's limousine drove by and stopped at the gates ahead. The gates swung open and the limo drove through. The guards walked back to their original spots.

"Boss, I think Vencenti just drove in. We await your orders," Arron said through his mouthpiece.

"Stand down for a moment," Michael said.

"Damn it to hell," Michael said as he pondered the next course of action. He looked at those around him. He could see they felt his peril but waited patiently. Michael pulled out his cell phone and dialed the mansion.

"Put Mr. Vencenti on, this is Canon."

"Michael, I don't know if I want to hear what you have to say."

"I'll make it brief. I know he's there with you. This doesn't have to go all the way," Michael urged.

"There are no options here Michael. Let's end this."

"Obviously you will not send him out?"

"I must stand on what I said before."

"As you put it once before, as one warrior to another, I would ask you to move to a part of your home that will give you a safe haven. I will be coming for Tony very soon and there is no reason for you to be harmed. I have given that order to my associates. I only want your Godson."

There was a silence on the phone.

"I will not be available when you come," Angelo said, then hung up.

"Team one you are a go," Michael said as he put his cell down.

"On three, two, one," Arron said, as he pulled the trigger. Both men fell backwards away from the driveway and laid still. Kennedy and Chad moved to the right around the wall that surrounded the estate. Arron and Brian moved to their left. One by one the two teams dropped six more guards without any lethal shots being fired. Just as Michael and his team started to move up his cell phone rang. He hesitated for a moment then answered it.

"Michael this is Sommers. I'm in town and I know what's happening. If you're going where I think you might you need to stop and reconsider."

"You had your chance. Your friends Kohl and Lima decided to make names for them and you see where that got them. How much of a part in that did you play?"

"I wasn't here Michael, I just now found out about it."

"I'm going to be busy for awhile Clay. You're not part of this now," Michael said, then hung up.

"We have them sir. They're at Collins and Ocean View drive."

"Where does Angelo Vencenti live?"

"I have it here, 23565 Ocean View Drive."

"Roll two S.W.A.T. teams and four assault units to that address. Tell them this is an ATF priority operation and to stand down until I arrive. This is a silent run; code one. They are not to go in," Sommers ordered.

Michael put his cell phone in his pocket and said, "Let's go."

Stacy pulled up with fifteen feet of the main gate with the lights off. Mason got out in full gear and went to the center of the gate. He placed a shape charge on the locking mechanism then quickly came back to the Escalade. R.C. and Dawson Larch's teams pulled up next to them in the other Escalades and waited.

R.C. flipped the switch and the charge fired blowing the gates apart and inward. Dawson was the first to go in followed by R.C. then Stacy. Dawson continued around the drive to the rear of the mansion.

They began taking fire from several men that appeared from the balcony above. Once Michael, Jim, and Mason exited, Stacy turned the Escalade around and headed it back towards the gate. She cocked her 9mm as she stayed in the SUV.

As Michael approached the front door one man came out only to be taken down by one shot to the thigh and one in his calf by Jim. As Mason got to him the man was reaching for his dropped .45. Mason kicked him in the jaw, knocking him unconscious. Jim and Mason went into the foyer together and took fire from two men in the living room and one in the hallway off to Jim's left. Mason laid down a two-second burst and hit one of the men as the other dove for cover. Lamps and end tables shattered and books from the bookcase shredded from the pulse cannon's onslaught. Michael could hear gunfire from the outside as he walked forward a few steps. Jim fired his automatic four times down the hallway then laid on the floor and waited. The baited shooter down the hallway came out to fire again and Jim laid in a four shot pattern which dropped him permanently. Mason went to the right after the man he missed. Jim and Michael walked slowly towards the main hall where he had met Angelo for the first time.

From the glass doors straight ahead of them two men appeared and fired their automatic rifles sending Michael and Jim diving for cover. Jim took a round in the thigh just above the kneecap. He rolled against the wall in pain as blood shot out covering his hands. It didn't break the bone but the pain was unbearable. He pulled his belt off and tied it tight at the wound. He backed up against the wall as the two fired another volley. The chair next to him splintered and moved several feet from him. Michael rose up and fired five rounds hitting one of the men who then crashed through the window behind. Michael ejected the clip from his 9mm and slammed in another. Michael told Jim to stay put and watch the entrance. Jim pulled his clip out of his automatic and seeing he had two bullets left he reached for another just as someone stepped out the door to his left which Michael had just passed. As the figure took aim at Michael, Jim reached down to his right calf and drew two knives. In an off balanced motion he threw them both, hitting the figure who cried out. One knife went into the back of his right arm above the elbow and the second below the elbow in his forearm. The figure dropped his automatic at the same time Michael turned around. The man lunged back into the doorway. "Sarino," Michael yelled as he fired four rounds into the door opening.

Mason was having trouble stalking his target. It was another minute before they heard the unmistakable sound of a three-second burst from his pulse cannon. Glass shattered and yells came echoing through the house. Michael felt like he was at the police target range as he walked slowly, first pointing up to the second story balcony then back down to the doors and windows around him. As he turned to walk to his right another figure appeared on the balcony above him and fired four times hitting Michael twice in the back. Michael dropped face first into the sofa pillows then down to the floor.

"I got em Tony. I got him, he's down," Sal Danza said as he fired twice more to make sure.

Jim wasn't at the right angle to fire but Mason was. Another burst from the pulse cannon literally ripped Sal apart as he flew back into the wall. Mason came to Michael's side just as automatic fire once again came from the far patio entranceway. Mason was hit twice and Michael once. The Kevlar jackets and shirts had kept them alive. Mason fired again and then made his way across the room to the patio doors. Michael sat up, put his back against the sofa and cocked his 9mm. The sting of a thousand fire ants surrounded the places he had been hit. The flower vase on the coffee table next to Michael shattered as Sarino and Pete Batti, one of his triggermen, ran into the room and took cover. Michael stayed low and backed up through the room. He fired a half dozen rounds as the two figures moved across the room towards him. Michael and Sarino fired six rounds at each other but only

Sarino was hit in his left forearm. Both Sarino and Batti made a run for the parlor to their right. Sarino made it and Jim shot Batti three times, sending him into the parlor door and down to the floor. It was now quiet, both in and outside of the mansion. Mason came into view at the far right of the room. Michael told him to get Jim out of here.

"You're supposed to be so good Canon, how come you have men lying everywhere? What is it now, just you and me?" Sarino said as he fired six rounds in Michael's direction. Michael fired three times then his automatic jammed. The last round hit Sarino in the upper right chest and he cried out. He looked around and there was only one man near him, dead on the floor. As he headed for him Sarino fired off three rounds forcing Michael flat on the floor. Michael crawled to the man and grabbed his shotgun. He stood up next to the fireplace as Sarino fired three times more. The last bullet from Sarino's gun ricocheted off the stone fireplace catching Michael through the inside left wrist, imbedding itself deep into his forearm. The pain shot through him like a hot poker. The bullet severed a vein and he began to bleed profusely. He knew Sarino had a revolver and had to reload after every six times he fired. Michael walked carefully back to his right, following Sarino's voice, then stopped. He stood quietly in pain as he pushed his left arm into his stomach to stop the bleeding. A shotgun hung straight down at his right side. He watched through the mirror on the back of the parlor door, as his bleeding adversary dropped to his knees. Sarino reached into his jacket pocket and slapped a handful of .38 cartridges on the floor in front of him. Vencenti and four of his men had quietly come out and stood unnoticed to Michael's right at the second floor railing.

"You know my godfather said you were a dangerous man. This just goes to show you he doesn't know shit," Sarino said, having trouble loading the .38 with only his right hand. "He was always the man, always the one they bowed to, well not anymore. I fixed all that."

"You're finished Sarino. Your little reign of terror is over," Michael said as he continued to watch.

"My godfather doesn't know it but he's next on the list. He never gave me a chance but I fixed him," Tony said, spitting out blood on the floor. "That whore he had come to the house for years, yeah, she was his downfall. It did me good to see her die slowly from the needle I slid into her arm," he said laughing. "The big man was sleeping like a baby from the sedative the organizer gave him."

Tony struggled to close the cylinder.

"What can I say, at least I'm gonna walk into prison. That's something your girlfriend whore can't say," Tony uttered as he stood up.

Sarino walked to his left back to the sofa and then raised his gun when he saw Michael standing there.

Michael raised his shotgun and fired twice, point blank into Sarino's legs cutting them out from under him. As he fell Michael walked towards him. Sarino's screams in agony echoed throughout the house as he use his arms to roll over. As he raised the .38 again Michael fired one last time taking his chest back through his spine. Michael's head was ready to burst from the adrenaline rush he just experienced. He stood there for a moment, then turned and started to walk back to the door. He stopped as Vencenti appeared in front of him flanked by his men.

"I never thought it would go this far Michael," Vencenti said as he looked past Michael at his grandson lying dead.

"I came to you for help and you sent me away," Michael stated. "Only one question remains. Do we have a problem?"

Vencenti stood quietly for a moment as he recollected what he heard from the balcony.

"I gave him everything."

"Do we have a problem Mr. Vencenti?" Michael repeated in a slightly stronger tone of voice.

"No Michael, we have no problem between us."

As Michael took his first step Vencenti and his men looked behind them to see Mason and Kennedy in full battle gear holding their pulse cannons straight up towards the ceiling. They waited until Michael walked by then followed him out the door.

Stacy was there to meet them and put her arm around Michael. She steadied him as they walked to the Escalade.

From the road below several floodlights came on lighting up the entire area around them. Michael's cell phone rang as he sat in the door. R.C., Dawson, Steve, and Brian came up close to Michael.

"Michael this is Sommers. It's over. I'm asking you to throw your weapons down."

"I agree it's over but you have to remember, this isn't happening," Michael said, as Stacy and Steve wrapped his arm.

"Just lay everything down, walk away from the truck and nobody will be hurt," Sommers said.

"Clay, take a moment and look around you. Look at your men. Look at the homes full of people. You know what we can do. You saw it first hand in Salt Lake. I can wipe out a three-block radius of this neighborhood with what we have in the trucks. I don't think you want that."

"I'm not going to fall for one of your bluffs Michael. I know you don't have anything, and if you did you wouldn't kill a lot of innocent people. You have your own people to think about."

"What, to die in prison because of a politician's rules or die as a team for what you and I both know is right."

"Even if you had something you won't do it Michael. If Stacy is there, let me speak to her."

"Yes, Mr. Sommers."

"Stacy, you're a sensible woman, talk to him. You have everything to live for."

"You've never understood, Mr. Sommers. Michael is doing what had to be done. Whatever he says will be carried out without question. Please listen to him."

"Mason, Steve, set the timers for sixty seconds. They can't get to us before they implode," Michael said as he made sure Sommers heard.

"Damn you to hell Michael. Timers for what?"

"Two small fusion bombs. They will level this entire hillside before you can get to us. Call it Clay. You can make this all go away."

"Michael, I have to assume you got what you came after. What is it you want?"

"Move your men back, even the ones behind us. Remember what I told you in Salt Lake, none of this ever happened. You have thirty seconds Clay. Don't press me."

"Where did we get bombs?" R.C. asked Mason.

Mason just shrugged his shoulders.

"Get everybody back in the Escalades and get ready to move," Michael said as he waited.

The police cars began moving from behind the mansion from both directions.

"Michael, this never happened. Take your people home," Clay said.

As Stacy turned around and followed the other Escalade out the gate and down the hill, Michael could see Sommers men running up the grounds of the mansion towards the house. Sommers might have been slow to get things done but he wasn't stupid. He knew Michael and the Ranger's capabilities. He knew he couldn't call Michael's bluff.

* *

Stacy drove to the hospital as the other two teams went back to the lodge to get ready to fly out. Steve had a gurney brought out for Jim who was holding his own. Stacy walked with Michael to the emergency room. Mason and Steve stayed outside the glassed in room and watched the entrance for any trouble. Stacy took the elevator up and got out on Tamara's floor.

"Stacy, my God what happened? You're bleeding," Tamara said, as she sat up in bed.

"I'm all right, it's Michael's blood."

Tamara grabbed her and half yelled.

"Whoa, take it easy. He's going to be fine; he's in the ER right now."

Tamara was shaking as Stacy held her and then talked of the confrontation.

"Help me in my chair," Tamara said. "Is it over?"

"Oh yeah, we can go home now."

* *

It took them about thirty minutes before the last bandage was clipped on Michael's arm. He could see they were nearly finished with Jim too. He left with Mason and Steve and headed up to see Tamara.

Tamara was in tears as Michael knelt next to her and put his right arm around her. Doctor Wallace was called and he came right over. Michael talked with him in his office.

"You should feel relieved we will be out of your hair tomorrow."

"Michael, you can't know how much. You certainly know how to test the procedures of an ER," Jon said as he slid a cup of coffee over to him.

"I am truly sorry for all the rules you had to break to do what you did for us. I'm trying to think of a way to repay you."

"Well, I might be removed from my position but I hope not. However, if I were fired I would probably come and work for you. Hell, following you guys around would give me all the work I needed."

They had a quiet laugh.

The shift nurse came in and handed Jon a small bottle and then left.

"Here, take one or two of these if the pain comes back. Just don't drive, ok?"

"Thanks Jon. When can I take my favorite girl home?"

"She's yours anytime you want her. She has a portfolio of everything related to her condition. I can't say I'm going to miss you Michael," Jon said as he came around his desk and they shook hands. "Call me sometime and let me know how you're doing."

Michael assured him he would then went back to see Tamara. Michael said they would be back in the morning to take her out of there. She couldn't wait.

* *

Stacy drove the team back after Kennedy arrived for the night shift. Michael couldn't help but smile at his dedication.

When they arrived back at the lodge everybody greeted them with handshakes and hugs. Michael could see the exhaustion in all of them as R.C. brought him a drink.

"Michael, you told Sommers we had something that could wipe out three square blocks. We really didn't, did we?" R.C. asked. "You're supposed to tell me about these things."

"Why don't I just keep that my secret Richard?" Michael said, then winked at Stacy. After all, anything had to be better than eating one of your barbequed hamburgers again."

The place erupted in laughter as R.C. came over and ran his knuckles into Michael's head.

"You just wait until you get well. I'm gonna whip your ass."

The built up tension and anxiety went right out the window from watching R.C. getting the short end again. When it quieted down Michael said a few words.

"My friends, we came through to live another day. I know I brought you in on my vendetta and you came through for Tamara and me. I would have to work twenty lifetimes to repay all of you for your dedication and loyalty."

They raised their glasses and toasted Michael. Shortly after, Michael and Stacy left. She opened his door and helped him off with his jacket.

"Guess what? When I called C.J. to tell him we were all right, a gal answered. It was Yvonne, one of my new pit crew workers that helps C.J. with his truck when I'm running. I could hear the shower running."

"I'm sorry Stacy. I guess I've ruined it for you bringing you down."

"Actually it's a blessing in disguise. He and I never slept together so I have nothing to miss or look forward to."

"Could you get me two of those pills in my jacket pocket?"

"Sure. Anything else I can do for you Michael?"

"No I've got it from here, go get some sleep."

"Ok, night Boss."

Chapter 52

The rising sun burnt off the last of the night's dampness. R.C. and the team loaded everything on the Galaxy cargo plane. They were getting ready to depart. Another pilot was bought in to take the Falcon and some of the team back. The Escalade and the Lincoln drove up and stopped. R.C. and Steve carried Tamara on board the Challenger 6 as others helped Jim, Paul, and Ernie aboard. The Escalade was put on the Galaxy and the Lincoln remained with the keys in the ignition as they requested at the rental office.

As Jeff leveled off at their cruising altitude, Molly brought them all something to snack on. Stacy sat next to Jim and bent his ear all the way back with racing talk.

"Boss, R.C. said to give this to you," Mason said handing Michael a small bust of Julius Caesar.

Michael smiled and handed it to Tamara.

"He said not to drop it. It's worth somewhere in the neighborhood of fifteen million dollars."

The rest of the flight took on a new meaning.

Chapter 53

The sun began to shine through the bedroom window of Michael's suite at the Conquistador Hotel and Casino. He opened his eyes and saw Tamara lying there looking at him.

"I know I look terrible in the morning."

"You look like someone I could live with my entire life, even though you snore when you're tired," she said with a smile.

He slid over the distance between them and she raised her head as he put his arm under it.

"You feel good," he said, then kissed her good morning.

He could feel her wanting to roll into him so he lifted her shoulder as she put her hand down along her right leg. He gently pulled her and she molded right into him with little effort. She felt good to him as he ran his hand across her shoulders and back as far as he could with only one good arm.

"Is this the blind leading the blind or what," she said as she let her hands rub his face and chest?

They laughed quietly but just being able to touch each other again made it all right. A half hour later he called room service for a continental breakfast and an in-bed tray. He got up and put a towel around him. Within minutes a cart was wheeled in and he tipped the young man. Tamara sat up and he put pillows behind her back. He managed to get the wide tray across her then slid in next to her as she held the tray. They again laughed at their predicament as they enjoyed their first breakfast alone in a long time.

"We have to get moving, we're due to have company."

"Who?" Tamara asked.

"Catherine is flying up this morning. I want somebody with you when I'm not here."

"Michael that's wonderful. I was going to talk to you about that. Go get ready."

He kissed her then headed for the shower. Holding his left arm out of the water was a task but made for a quicker shower. He dressed then came out. He stood there in amazement. Tamara was sitting in the wheelchair fully dressed.

"What took you so long?" she said with a big smile.

"Look at you, I mean you are something."

"Of course I am. I'm fully functional; my only problem is I just can't walk yet."

Five minutes later brought a knock on the door. Catherine and Kennedy came in. Hugs went around. Michael said he needed to go to the office.

"Not like that you're not," Catherine said, picking up a small case. "Come in the bathroom."

His arm had bled considerably and she removed the bandage. Within minutes she had replaced the staple over the incision and re-bandaged his arm.

"Now you two go do whatever it is you do and let us ladies get some work done," Catherine said, then gave Kennedy a big kiss.

"So Shawn, you don't mind me bringing her up do you?"

"Boss, I could have fallen over when she told me. I want to thank you."

"No, I want to thank you, my friend, for sticking by my side these years. She is very important to you and I couldn't be happier for you both."

"The entire team will always be there when you need us, me especially. We have been through things they only write about in fiction books. I wouldn't have missed those times for anything in the world."

"Me neither."

Chapter 54

Several weeks went by. Tamara had something to talk to Michael about as he sat across from her in a chair. She told him she had called her friend Kai Li in Kobe, Japan several times. They talked about what had happened in her life. Kai Li suggested going to a retreat located in northern California to seek help from those there. The trip might only last a week but she wanted to hear his opinion before making her decision.

"Michael, I have seen their healing arts first hand growing up. They use the old methods, not these that need scientific proof before they can be used. Having Doctor Ambler there for me was more than I could have asked for but he tried. I would like to do this. If it doesn't work out then at least we know and can get on with our lives."

Michael leaned over and kissed her.

"I've had thoughts along the same lines. I think it would be a wonderful idea and I support you in this. I'd like to go with you to if that's all right."

She took his hand as he wheeled her to the sofa.

"It was asked that I go first. They also think it's a good idea for you to be there, but I'll need a couple of days first. I am so happy you will do this with me. Stacy will go to help me and they asked for you to come after two days."

Michael totally understood and thought about nothing else over the two days she was gone.

* *

The Falcon 2 touched down at the small airport outside Crystal Lake shortly after dawn. Renting a car he drove to the retreat located northeast of the town about forty miles away. The retreat was nestled within the forest below a snow-capped mountain that seemed to reach to the heavens. He stood in awe at the grandeur of the retreat's surroundings. Soon he was met by two priests. The three walked for nearly fifteen minutes. Several temples and houses of the Asian culture stood before him.

"Welcome Michael, I am Yukio. Please come this way for some refreshments."

They walked down into a perfectly manicured garden to a stone table with two cups on it.

"How are Tamara and Stacy?"

"They are well. You will see them soon."

Just then a butterfly came down and sat on Michael's thumb. He held his hand steady for a moment then lifted it slowly. "It's beautiful."

"I see the gentleness Tamara spoke of. That is a wonderful thing from the heart."

"It is truly beautiful here Yukio."

"This exists in all places but we tend to not see it. Michael, I can see you are a very deep person in thought and body. I have walked with both Tamara and Stacy. Please walk with me and tell me about you from the first thing you can recall as a child to the present. I realize this is asking a lot so quickly, but it will be very important in understanding Tamara's condition."

Picking up their cups of water they started slowly up a narrow path that lead towards the mountains. Yukio listened without comment as Michael told him of his life and those that had come into it and left. They sat down several times over the next two hours as Michael was able to write his autobiography in words. Yukio never spoke a word until Michael had finished. They sat by a small waterfall.

"How do you feel physically Michael?"

"I'm tired. Not from the walk, but just from talking."

The mental burden you have carried for others has made its presence in your physical body. Now you are preparing to bring Tamara into your mind and body and I sense reservation."

"I would give everything I possess if I could just see her whole again."

"She is not in want of the material things of the world. She has the want of everything you possess in your mind and heart."

"Yukio, I wasn't speaking of material things, I was speaking of giving my life for hers, to see her walk again," Michael said as he put his head in his hands.

"For this to happen there is a burden that you carry that must be brought out from within you. You have already spoken of it as we walked. I will help you to understand it."

"Maybe I have been cursed for what I have done since I lost my family."

"Your actions of conscious have been justified within you. Michael, do you believe in an afterlife?"

"I want to believe there is one."

"When you honor the resting place of your lost loved ones do you not tell them you will see them one day?"

"Yes, every time I go. They shouldn't have been there. I maybe could have prevented it from happening."

"From that you know you will see them. They may have left the physical world but in your heart they will never leave. Just knowing and believing in that will suppress the demon you have created within yourself. Come, let us go back."

As they walked, Yukio talked of attempting to bring his life back into balance. A balance that Tamara has to face ten-fold.

"How can Stacy and I help her?"

Yukio smiled. "Often I am honored with the feelings of two people with enough love to overcome life. Now I am with three who share a bond of equal love for one another. I too must watch and learn."

"Are Tamara and Stacy linked in life someway?"

"Yes, and you are also, to both of them. One of you will find another path to follow in time, as your life has. This is something that is meant to be. Who will leave cannot be foretold. The question of your love for them was answered when we first met. You put them above yourself as they both did for you."

"What will I do now that I'm here?"

"We will rest your body and relax your mind. Your physical presence with the two of them is as important as is your mental awareness of them. Take some time to reacquaint yourself with them and later we will share food together."

Yukio escorted Michael to one of the smaller dwellings. Michael went inside alone and found Tamara and Stacy sitting and talking. Stacy met him with a hug. Tamara had tears in her eyes as he held her tightly.

"I have missed you so," Tamara said then kissed him repeatedly.

Tamara talked of Yukio and the others that were trying to understand her physical problem. After talking to

Yukio at length, Michael was now beginning to see and understand the bond the three of them shared.

Over the next two days the three shared the baths of the natural hot springs nearby. Yukio talked to each of them individually, at least twice a day. The natural order was now being felt by the three of them. The last day brought news they had hoped to be of a more positive nature. Though Tamara had repaired her mind, her body would have to take its own course to find balance. Michael had finally learned peace with himself, Susanne, Jennifer, and Chris. Everything the three had conquered individually and together was accepted in a new light as they said goodbye to Yukio. The Falcon 2 waited for them at the airport to take them back to the city.

Chapter 55

The next week enabled Michael to continue with his plans for the company. The Army was ecstatic with the planes and another order was forth coming. Monica stopped by to pick up R.C., but he wasn't ready to go so she went to see Michael.

"You gonna offer a lady a drink cowboy?" she said as she stuck her head in the door.

"Monica, this is so great. Come on in."

He gave her a hug and a kiss. After he fixed them a drink they talked for a few minutes on the futon by the window.

"Monica, we've gone out of business."

"Oh Michael, I thought Aero was doing great. I mean R.C. said it was."

"No sweetheart, I mean the other business."

She hugged him.

"Thank you Michael. Does Richard know?"

"No, I don't want to disillusion him. He likes to think of adventure so bursting his bubble would be wrong. That's just between you and me."

"You are so right. Listen Michael, I need to tell you something but I don't want to hurt you."

"Go ahead."

"Andrea's engaged to be married."

"I couldn't be happier for her and I mean that from my heart."

"I know you do. That's why you are you and I love you for that."

"Who do you love? Are you talking about me again?" R.C. said as he came in.

"No, I love Michael."

Michael winked at R.C.

"That's ok but who are you going home with?" he said as he gave her a kiss.

"Well you of course, Michael can't barbeque like you do," she said, then winked at Michael.

They left. Michael went to a meeting with several travel agents that specialized in island vacation packages. Sending a list around to the team with R.C., Michael asked them to choose a seven-day vacation spot. They could bring anyone with them they chose, or could come as a single. It would be first-class all the way. The majority of them chose Hawaii. Some chose Nassau in the Grand Bahama chain. Michael finished signing papers and contracts with Marsha that would clear his schedule. He was getting a two-week start on the others, vacation-wise.

* *

At daybreak, Michael and Tamara flew out of McCarran on the Falcon 2. They headed to Dallas where they did a courtesy refueling before heading on to West Palm Beach. From there it was less than an hour hop to the airport at North Eleuthera Island where a rental car awaited them. Ernie and the crew flew back to Nassau Island where they planned an entire week of activities.

Michael and Tamara took the villa at the very end of the island. It was a two bedroom, two-bath villa with a 180-degree view of the Caribbean. Tamara was totally taken as she looked at the vaulted ceiling and huge living and dining area. The kitchen was equipped with full-sized appliances right down to a washer and dryer. Michael could feel her excitement as she wheeled herself from room to room. Now they had the privacy they wanted.

Michael took full advantage of the vacation package by having meals prepared for them. Even though the refrigerator and cupboards were well stocked with everything they needed, a local woman Cara, and her daughter Cassandra, fixed them lunch daily. With the exception of a few nights, they returned each evening to prepare a nice dinner. Nothing was rushed so they could enjoy everything.

"You know what I'd like to do right now my darling."

"Go back home?"

"No silly, I would like to feel the water on my body. What do you say; want to get wet with me?"

He smiled and kissed her.

The sun was just setting and the moon was beginning its dominant presence behind them. He wheeled her to the end of the walkway. With the water's edge about forty yards in front of them he picked her up and carried her across the warm sand.

"I have to weigh a ton. I don't want to hurt your arm."

"A ton…no."

She pinched his chest at his slow remark, which got him laughing. Walking out into the water waist deep he let her down while still holding on to her lightly. She treaded water for a few minutes then laid her head back and floated. He slowly pulled her in a circle as she felt the water's warm massaging touch. She asked him to put his hand in the small of her back to hold her. She unsnapped her top and laid it around his neck. The bottom of her suit snapped at the side and it came off next. He continued to hold her as she brought the water up over her. Twinges of sexual longing began to flash through him when he kissed her stomach and her breasts as she ran her hands through his hair. She was so beautiful, he thought, as he let his mind absorb the water running over her features. She pulled him to her and held him as he moved in a small circle on the ocean floor.

"Isn't this what I promised you a long time ago?"

"Yes, you sure did."

They spent an hour in the warm stimulating water then he carried her back to shore. The rest of the evening was spent just being near one another. Their first night's sleep in paradise was like heaven.

They set up a daily routine of watching the sunrise from the beach then spending at least thirty minutes in the warm waters.

Over the next ten days the only change in their routine was the occasional rain shower about mid-afternoon. On those occasions, they both took a nap listening to the rain falling outside. They had visited shops and had purchased or rented items that made their trips to the water more fun. A four-wheeled scooter truck was Tamara's favorite because she could drive it on the beach by herself as Michael watched from his lounge. A swimming pool lounge chair with heavy foam allowed her to float as Michael massaged her lower body routinely in the water.

Something happened just before noon on the eleventh day that they would remember their entire lives. They had been lounging in four feet of water for nearly an hour. Michael pushed her floating lounge chair up to the water's edge. Her feet laid in several inches of water as the foaming waves surrounded her calves. He was kneeling next to her when she yelled out. "Ouch, Michael help me!"

"What, tell me?"

"Something's in the water, by my foot," she said, reaching down to her left leg.

He quickly moved around to her left side and lifted her foot. A small crab had latched onto her little toe with its pincher. Michael released its hold and set him down on the sand.

"Michael, I could feel it, I can feel you touching my toes," she said. He set her foot down in the water and held her. He couldn't believe it himself.

He set her on the four-wheeler and they went to the house. He carried her to the sofa where he brushed some sand from her feet with a dry washcloth. She could feel momentary twinges as he touched each toe and her left ankle. He touched every part of her legs and though the feelings were still void within them she did have feeling in her toes. That was a start.

"Maybe tonight we can be as one again my darling," she said as she kissed him.

Tamara wheeled herself out to the patio, excited about their experience.

"Michael I am so happy right now I haven't the words to tell you," she said as he brought her a drink. "I hope this is a start and not just a momentary thing."

"I read once that the chemical composition in our bodies is the same as the salt water in the oceans, or something like that. Why do I want to think your body is absorbing what it needs and is coming back into balance with itself?"

"That does make a lot of sense. I'm glad we came here. You always know what's best."

"It was your idea to come here if my memory serves me."

She looked at him with a blank stare for a moment then smiled. "That's right; I wanted to swim in the nude didn't I?"

"Any more subliminal messages going through that beautiful head of yours I should know about?"

"Maybe," she said. "Let's talk about them after the servants leave for the day."

"Oh, aren't we big time, when the servants leave."

"Well I am rich, I have you," she said as she laid her head on his shoulder.

Cara and Cassandra prepared a wonderful shellfish platter for them. Michael asked them to share dinner with them. It was a nice gesture and was gratefully accepted by the mother and daughter. After they had gone Tamara pulled herself onto the sofa and waited as Michael fixed them a drink. He sat down and she moved up on his lap. She liked him holding her as she put her head on his shoulder. She asked him about his engagement at Vencenti's mansion and Sommers' last stand. She listened intently like a child being told a fairy tale at bedtime would. When he finished she yawned then put her hand to her mouth.

"I'm sorry, I swear it's not the company, it must be late."

She used the larger bathroom and he utilized the other. When he came out she was lying in bed waiting for him. She asked him to leave the light on in the hallway. It gave some light to the bedroom but wasn't overpowering.

He picked up a small pillow from the sofa and threw it at the foot of the bed. He could tell from her breathing she was full of anticipation as she pulled him into her. Their hands rubbed each other's smooth body surfaces. He began to kiss her and slowly moved down to her breasts. She ran her fingers through his hair and like before, guided his head to areas that needed more attention. His own body fought hard to maintain control as he moved to her velvety flat stomach. He helped her roll away from him to her side. The small pillow he brought in fit perfectly against her buttocks. Slowly rolling her back onto the pillow brought her pelvis up to a different plane. He moved her legs apart slightly. His chest rubbed through her hair as he slid up and kissed her stomach. Even he could feel her upper body muscles tighten and relax as he slowly started back down.

The sensitivity in the one area of her he enjoyed kissing was still not fully responding. She pulled him back up to her. Thinking more sensitive areas may be up higher within her she gently put some lubrication on herself and then put him where his lips had just been. Carefully he began movements that quickly proved her theory right. She could feel him as he moved several inches inside her and it was like a switch being turned on. He sensed her every movement and she pulled on his shoulders with the forward rhythm he had begun. It took a while before she reached a peak she couldn't stop. The flood of static emotion shot through her at the same time Michael couldn't hold on any longer. She cried out being consumed by passion. He lay on top of her on his forearms and kissed her as their bodies unwound from the activity long since experienced. He slipped out and slid the pillow from beneath her. She lay still as he slowly ran his hand over her wet body. As he moved his hand down her right leg he could feel a slight warm dampness unlike the full wetness above her waist. He knew what nature was doing. They lay like that until they fell asleep.

Chapter 56

Inasmuch as they enjoyed their total privacy, Michael and Tamara had lunch then headed for the airport to meet the group from the team that decided to come over to Eleuthera for a week.

Michael wasn't sure if the islands would ban Americans from ever coming back after seeing R.C. walk off the Falcon 2. R.C. wore a flowered shirt so bright everyone donned sunglasses just to look at him. He also wore shorts with stripes, black oxfords, and long black socks up to the knee. Monica said he dressed that way on purpose to have some fun with everyone, but she guaranteed it would be a one-time thing. Michael had rented several villas next to theirs for the next two weeks and got everyone set up.

About mid-afternoon Michael donned shorts and a light pullover and Tamara dressed in a wrap-around skirt over her two-piece swimsuit. Michael wheeled Tamara down the walkway past the other villas to see what was going on. They could have made a movie of the crystal white beach meeting the light blue waters of the cove. The villas were about two hundred yards apart with a series of walkways connecting all of them.

R.C. and Monica were waist deep in the water splashing about as they passed their villa. They all waved. Michael couldn't believe how settled in Jim and Paul were as they stretched out on lounges taking in the sun's rays. Out of their villa came two gals in their early twenties in two-piece island wear bringing them drinks.

"Obviously I don't have to ask if you two need anything," Michael said as they stopped.

They shook hands and laughed at how tough they had it.

"Well Michael, you did say to enjoy everything and besides, Tiki and Kari have had some medical training. We might not heal up for weeks without them," Jim said smiling as he lifted his leg back up on the lounge.

"I don't think reading medical flyers in the doctor's office qualifies them as doctors," Michael commented.

That observation got them all laughing.

* * * * * * * * * * * * * * * * * * * *

The evening of day two found Michael and Tamara arriving at the casino for a planned dinner with everyone.

The lights and sounds as they went into the casino invigorated them both as the made their way to the main dining room. Thinking they would beat everyone quickly disappeared as everyone greeted them like long lost friends. They all ordered dinner, then drinks were served.

"I suppose you guys can't wait to go back to Seattle?" Michael asked Paul and Jim.

"Seattle, where's that?" Paul asked.

"Michael, we would like to thank you for all you've done for us. R.C. gave us another large check like before. I still have the feeling there is something not right with that but something else tells me we did something extraordinary for the good of it. Isn't that right?" Jim asked.

"The latter is what's important. I can't be prouder of you two and the others. I never imagined this could have happened either but one thing led to another and it kept escalating. Look where everything would be right now if we hadn't interceded. It's all over now and behind us."

He raised his glass and everyone toasted to the fact.

"I guess it will be kinda hard going back to a job where rules are volumes thick."

"We've all talked about the future. Several of us are going to leave the force and start over now that we have the means. None of us have any regrets for ourselves, only for those who we lost from the team."

"Nicely said Jim," Michael commented.

They toasted again.

Dinner was fantastic. Michael was very proud as he looked at all of them. They soon broke up and headed to the main casino. Tamara wasn't a gambler so she watched Michael at first play card games. They liked to observe other people too with their antics when winning and losing. Tamara finally found a dollar slot machine that started giving her something back. Neither of them could really tell exactly how they were winning because of the countless reel patterns. They were satisfied as the credits grew on the counter. Michael had put a hundred in to start them off and it was now up to over a thousand. She made him kiss her on any win of one hundred dollars or more. This added to the game's atmosphere. Their credits went up and down over the hour they played. They decided to quit when it got back up to one thousand dollars. Michael just smiled as an attendant paid Tamara her winnings. Her smile lit up the room.

They said good night to everyone and left for home. They had a drink on the patio then went to bed.

* *

Even though they all had gotten together on the sixth day for dinner again, day seven came too soon as they all met at the dock. First class tickets on the regular airlines would take them all home from Nassau. They watched the graceful Falcon 2 land as the next wave of team Canon tourists got off.

Chapter 57

As pre-arranged, Dawson and Brandon Larch brought their girlfriends Cynthia and Clarisse respectively. The ironic part of that foursome was the girls were sisters. Mason and Arron planned to do some serious snorkeling and fishing while there. Not surprising, the last one in the party was the free spirited Stacy. Michael knew he had his hands full now. He and Tamara would have to hide to get any peace for themselves.

Tamara asked Michael if Stacy could stay with them and he said yes. Though they stuck to their ocean routine, Michael found he had more free time on his hands, as Stacy and Tamara were almost inseparable.

Day two allowed Michael and R.C. to get in a round of golf with the Larch brothers. Surprisingly they were all pretty close in handicap and it made for an enjoyable round. The sisters went shopping everyday and Stacy and Tamara worked on their tans. Dinner for the party at the casino was a night they all savored.

"Dawson, Cynthia and Clarisse are wonderful ladies, I am proud for you and Brandon. I'm glad they wanted to come with you."

"Thank you Michael. Yes, we are very fortunate and we both couldn't be happier."

"Do I see a double wedding in the future; come on you can tell me," Michael said as he lit a small cigar.

"Now you're embarrassing me Boss. I know Brandon would in a minute but…"

"Are you afraid she'll bring you down a notch or too?"

Something struck Dawson funny in the way Michael asked the question. In his deep voice he laughed out loud. This got everyone looking at them. Michael kept smiling as he looked at Dawson who looked back at him then started laughing out loud again.

"What's going on down there?" Cynthia asked with a big smile.

"Dawson was just telling me about a secret he's planning for you."

Cynthia got up and went behind Dawson, bringing his head back into her breasts. "You can tell me sweetheart, what is it?"

"No I can't. Like Michael says, it's a secret."

She kissed him on the top of his head. As she walked back to her chair she said she would find out later tonight. Some of the other people around their table looked and smiled, as laughter filled the room. Michael stood up gave Dawson a little hug and they patted each other on the back. The rest of the night went back and forth like that.

Stacy didn't gamble at all so she, Michael, and Tamara said goodnight. Once they got home they all went back in the warm water of the ocean for about a half hour.

After Stacy said goodnight, Michael and Tamara laid there and listened to the night sounds of the island, which put them fast asleep.

* *

Michael woke up first and carefully slipped out of bed so as not to wake Tamara. He went to the kitchen and turned on the coffee. He jumped into the shower, shaved, dressed, and poured a cup of coffee. Everyone else was sleeping so he went out on the patio to think about everything that had happened and to plan the upcoming days.

The rest of the week continued as the first two days had. Michael could see a little improvement in Tamara's legs and he liked the thought of having time on their side for a change. Stacy was tearfully excited when they told her of the feelings she was experiencing. She mentioned to Michael in San Francisco that she felt responsible for this happening to Tamara. Tamara had stopped her from killed Barco. This was news that removed some burden from her conscience. He was glad Stacy and Tamara were so close. Michael got a chance to do some morning fishing with Mason and Arron which delighted them to no end. He even dozed off several times in the lounge chair watching them catch fish. There was something about the sun's warmth plus relaxing that could just about put him to sleep.

The last night on the island, Michael arranged for a fire on the beach with a catered luau. It couldn't have been more beautifully set up. Everyone elaborated on the fabulous time spent and wanted to arrange for this to happen every year. The idea was well taken since money was certainly no object. Monica's heart was full of love and happiness as she watched Michael and R.C. smoke cigars, cut up and laugh with one another. Her world evolved around both of them and nothing could have made her happier.

"How do you rate Boss? We only get a week down here in paradise and you get a month?" Brandon asked as drinks were brought to them all by the party staff.

"I happen to be in good standing with the boss at Canon Aero," Michael answered with a smile. "Hey Cynthia, did you ever find out Dawson's secret?"

She thought for a moment as everybody waited for the mystery answer. "That night we kinda got sidetracked," then she started to laugh. "But I have one more night to find out."

Michael was as good as R.C. when it came to making an outing special. Around eleven they all headed back to their villas.

Day seven mirrored the happenings of a week earlier. The tearful goodbyes and the welcomed hello's started the day. Tamara asked Stacy if she could stay on another week. Michael agreed, as her help with Tamara was invaluable.

Chapter 58

Michael and Stacy kept her to the full therapy session anyway. Exercising her legs and massages made Michael know, through feel, that she was improving. Tamara loved the fun infighting between them both, some of which she instigated herself. Deciding not to go for the last swim of the day, Tamara sat on the patio and watched as Michael struggled to open a beach chair on the sand. Tamara yelled at him to go in but he declined. Stacy swam for about ten minutes then came out and sat with him on the sand.

"You are absolutely driving me crazy Michael. I want you to ask her before I go."

"I want to but…"

"But what, I got the ring for you just like you asked. Come on, you can do it. Do it tonight," she said.

"Ok, give me a few minutes after we go in."

"Thank you Michael," she said as she brushed the sand from her suit.

Tamara went into the kitchen and poured them all some coffee. Michael ran a brush through his hair. He came out of the bathroom and Stacy motioned for him to stop. She handed him a small box from her bathrobe pocket.

"Do it," she said, then went out into the living room and sat on the sofa.

Tamara was sitting in her wheelchair with a smile as he neared her. He knelt down in front of her. He took hold of her hand and then took a deep breath.

"Tamara, it's very hard to express my love for you in just a few words. You've brought so much into my life, a life I want to share with you from this moment on. Will you marry me?"

"Michael, that was so beautiful."

She gripped his hand hard as he handed her the small box. Emotions flooded through her as she opened it. She lifted out a ring with the top beautifully shaped like the head of a cat. In the cat's eyes were two diamonds. Two more diamonds came down both sides. She put her arms out and he raised her up out of the chair and held her tightly.

"Yes my darling, from the day I first saw you, to now and forever."

She kissed him several times. Stacy got up and hugged Tamara. She held her arms out to Michael. Tamara let Michael go and Stacy hugged him tightly. Fear suddenly shot through Michael as the thought of Tamara standing there alone hit him. He grabbed for her but she was standing there by herself looking down at her legs. "Michael," she cried out. "Oh Michael." He put his arms on him and she bent her own knees as he sat her down in the chair. He ran his hands on her legs and could feel muscles twinge at his touch. He quietly thanked God for making her whole again.

As they got their emotions under control they finished their coffee and went to bed.

"Thank you for letting Stacy stay here with us, it's meant so much to me."

"I know it has. She wanted to help you in every way she could."

They decided they wouldn't tell anybody about Tamara's progress until the right moment. Michael knew when that moment would be. He held her until she fell asleep.

* *

The third week was a free week for the three of them as Stacy stayed on. Tamara and Michael decided on a wedding in four weeks back in the city. Stacy had helped some of her other girlfriends in the past with this sort of thing so she asked to spearhead the project. Michael had called Doctor Wallace during the week Tamara first had feeling in her toes which couldn't have made him more pleased. He now called and brought him up to date on her progress. Michael sat out on the patio sipping on some iced tea and watched with total enjoyment as his two little tough nuts wrote things on tablets on what the wedding should have.

"Darling, we've never picked a chapel or church for the wedding. There's going to be a lot of people there, any suggestions?"

"I was kind of thinking someplace like the Conquistador Hotel and Casino. They have rooms set up just for weddings and conventions. They could handle all the people."

Tamara looked at Stacy and then they smiled.

"Do you think you could handle that part of the wedding?"

"Sure will, and by the way, I could arrange for the music if you'd like."

Again the two looked at each other. "We hadn't gotten that far, but sure, you can do that too."

Over the next few days Michael contacted the Conquistador and talked with all of those involved with their undertaking. A fully catered dinner afterwards for at least one hundred people was also talked about.

* *

As the three lay on the soft sand working on their tans, Michael got some flashbacks of his confrontation with the owner of the club where he first heard Larry Courier. Ideas began entering his mind about the entertainment part of his job in the wedding.

"Michael, before you go and get us something cold to drink, would you put some lotion on my legs and back?" Tamara asked.

He smiled as he picked up the lotion and knelt on the blanket at her ankles. As he applied the cool liquid he watched as he touched her legs. Like before, his massage caused twinges of movement under her skin. He felt each one of them as he went up from her ankles to where her suit began. He felt the water therapy and the sun's constant warmth was doing what was needed.

As the sun was an hour from setting, Michael called Glamour Tours. He asked for his friend Artie Silverman.

"Michael, how the hell are you?"

"Great Artie, how's our boy Larry?"

"Michael, you have an eye for picking them. He is doing so well even I can't believe it. The older generation is going wild for his appearances."

"I couldn't be more proud of him. He just needed a second chance. I thank you for that. Listen, I need him for a very special occasion coming up soon. How does he look schedule-wise?"

Michael gave him the date and location. There wouldn't be a problem.

* * * * * * * * * * * * * * * * * * * *

A nice dinner started the evening off and they just lounged around afterwards. Tamara and Stacy showed Michael all the things they were planning. They were getting invitations made from a company they located on the internet using Michael's laptop. Stacy found the CD player and CD's Tamara had at the hospital and asked if she could listen to some of them. Tamara brought them in case she had some free time for listening. Stacy walked to the beach and started singing along with some of the songs. Michael and Tamara finished looking at outfits she would like to wear for the wedding. He was relieved she wanted to keep it casual and not have the big dress with the mile long train.

Michael poured two coffees and met her on the patio. He put his arm around her as they watched Stacy swinging her arms as if she were dancing.

"I love that song she's singing," Tamara said as Stacy was within thirty feet of them.

They both started humming right along with her until she neared the end and stopped moving in the sand, *"...and when you're in love, it's the most wonderful time of the year."*

She had a beautiful voice but when she did a crescendo up to the last high note and held it, chills went through them both. They looked at each other as the echo faded away.

"I didn't know she could sing like that," Michael said as they applauded her loudly.

She bowed to them then shut off the player. She came back up and sat between them.

"I know you think I'm too young to know those songs but my mother always played them and I would sing along. I actually sang that one in my high school talent show and did pretty good."

"Did you win?"

"Hell no, one of the high school cheerleaders swinging her skinny butt and baton won. She really was lousy at cheerleading too."

They laughed.

"I'm going to fix some more coffee. Would you like some my beautiful Mrs. Canon."

"God I love that name, Mrs. Canon. Yes, I'd like a cup."

She patted him on his butt as he left the patio.

It was Stacy that had gone deep inside herself to help Tamara with her own locked away inadequacies and horrors, in all aspects of being in a relationship. Tamara had completely shut out the touch of a man after being sexually brutalized by two men after she had gotten inebriated in her teens. She had been labeled an iceberg in the Marines and had hurt several fellow marines who tried to force their way on her. It wasn't until she met Michael that the iceberg within her began to melt. Even though she knew he had Andrea, it was he who made her womanly instincts begin stirring again. Meeting Stacy at Aero and becoming close friends brought even more life into her.

The closer they got and the things they did together, the more she thought of Michael. The way in which Andrea left was a total shock to Tamara. Even still, it was Michael she began to love in her own private world of fantasy. In that world she could never be hurt. Then he came to San Francisco. She knew that in a month's time she would be giving him everything she possessed.

Chapter 59

On Saturday the last wave of Canon's tourists arrived and the week proceeded like before. The second day Michael walked down the beach with Marsha, his life long friend and personal secretary. They watched as Harry, her husband, flew by on a speedboat-towed parasail. They returned his wave as he went by.

"You know Michael, I haven't seen Harry this relaxed and excited for years. I am so glad you talked me into this."

"I should have sent you down here long before now. You deserve more times like these. You're even getting some sun," he said as he walked with his arm around her shoulders.

"Now I know you Michael, what did you bring me out here for other than to talk about Harry and me? What's up? You have a different look about you."

"Well, I want you to divorce Harry and marry me."

She dug her fingers into his side and they laughed. "Will you be serious, talk to me?"

"I haven't even told R.C. this but I'm going to marry Tamara Garrett in two weeks."

She stopped, turned, and hugged him tightly. She began to cry as she held him. Harry flew back by and yelled something down at them. She raised her arm and waved him off. Michael gave her his handkerchief as she pulled away.

"Michael I have lived for this day ever since we lost Susanne and the kids. I may never stop crying. My boy is getting married, I am so happy."

"Hey, save some for the wedding."

"I was so saddened by Tamara being paralyzed in that job accident. Those things just shouldn't be able to happen."

"There she is now."

Stacy was taking Tamara for a stroll in her wheelchair. Tamara had some soft drinks in a cooler on her lap and offered them one. Marsha hugged her tightly.

"I am so glad you have won Michael's heart. My son is finally leaving the nest."

"Are you Michael's…"

Marsha laughed and wiped her eyes again. "I've always thought of Michael as the son I never had. Now maybe he will stop asking me to divorce Harry and marry him."

Their laughter changed the moment.

"I'm going to walk mom home. See you two in a little while," Michael said laughing as Marsha pinched him.

Marsha hugged Stacy and Tamara, then they headed back down the beach.

When Michael returned he sat with Tamara on the sofa. She sat on his lap by herself. She put her head on his shoulder as he held her.

"There is nobody that doesn't love you my darling. Marsha is such a wonderful person. I wish I hadn't been in the wheelchair."

"I know but we talked about that. We have a time for you to lose the chair forever and that time depends on you getting better."

"I know but I just feel I can almost do that now."

Stacy came out of the bathroom and said she was going to the post office and the airport to pick up the packages they had ordered. As they watched her drive away they looked at each other and smiled.

"Yes, alone at last," Michael said.

They headed to the bedroom.

Stacy got back at the same time Cara and Cassandra arrived to prepare dinner. Tamara and Stacy opened the packages that contained the invitations and place cards. Michael went out and sat on the patio. He lit a cigarette and put his feet up. A lot of thoughts still flashed through his mind about the past several years. Being there in the islands had been the perfect fantasy shelter from harm. He didn't dread going back into the world of reality again as he had now become one with himself. Though one chapter in his life was ending, another one was just beginning and that made him feel alive.

* * * * * * * * * * * * * * * * * * * *

They saw everyone off the following Saturday morning. Michael flew back to the city for a few days as Tamara and Stacy continued to work on the wedding. He concluded all the contract paperwork at Aero and was now semi-free at last. He spent several hours working with the hotel manager and staff at the Conquistador Hotel. Lunch with Artie from Glamour Tours was long overdue.

* * * * * * * * * * * * * * * * * * * *

Larry Courier was doing several side stage spots in the city at the Sierra West Casino and was becoming popular. Michael went to see him, arriving an hour before Larry was to go on.

"Mr. Canon, so good to see you, he said as they shook hands.

"It's Michael. I hear you are doing all right for yourself. I just had lunch with Artie."

"Michael, you can't believe what you've done for my life. Doors are opening for me all over. I owe you."

Two soft drinks were brought to them.

"Do you have family or ever been married Larry?"

"I was married once, for a year, right out of college. Since then, I just date around. I know that special one is out there but so far she hasn't come along. Which reminds me, congratulations again to you and Tamara. I can't wait to sing for you. Thank you for asking me."

"You're welcome. Listen, I want to kick something by you and tell me what you think."

He talked with Larry for another thirty minutes on ideas for the wedding. Larry was excited as they laughed at what Michael was planning. The secret was theirs.

Chapter 60

Michael flew back to the islands in time for dinner. They couldn't be happier to see him and to hear what he had been doing. Tamara's progress was amazing as Stacy kept her to her strict routine. He brought Stacy some new CD's and she headed out to get the player. After dinner Michael and Tamara sat on the patio and listened to Stacy sing bits and pieces of the new songs he had brought.

"I am amazed at her voice range. She can really sing. I wonder why she never pursued a singing career?"

"She told me she was never able to afford it. She can sing anything you ask her to though," Tamara answered.

They applauded her as she finished on a high note that she held for about ten seconds, then fell backwards onto the sand.

"Are you getting excited?"

"Michael, I can't sleep thinking about it. I don't know if I can do it."

"It's easy, you just walk down, lay a few words on me, promise to obey, and we're out of there."

She tickled him and they started laughing.

"They don't say that obey stuff anymore, you're making that up."

She held him close but kept laughing quietly at the idea of what he said."

"Ok, if I have to agree to obey then I'm going in armed."

"You would, wouldn't you?"

"I was going to do it anyway just in case you decided to back out."

"Are you sure you only want Stacy as your maid of honor?"

"Yes, Stacy is all I want. How about you, is R.C. you're your only one?"

"You bet. I can't wait for you to see us. Remember what he was wearing the first day he got here, well…"

"There's no way, Michael C. Canon. You are not wearing that outfit," she said laughing out loud. She jumped on his lap and started wrestling with him.

"What does the C stand for in your middle name Michael?" Stacy asked as Tamara pulled herself together.

"I'm not sure. The story goes my mother wanted it to be Clarence and my father wanted Clifford and they never could come to an agreement, so it remained just C," Michael said as he started to go inside.

Tamara looked at Stacy then a Michael who finally couldn't hold the smile back.

"You're making that up Michael," Tamara said as they went after him. They caught him in the kitchen.

Chapter 61

They flew out on the Falcon 2 two days before the wedding. The hotel's own limousine picked them up at the airport and took them straight to the hotel. The red carpet was out for them as the owner and several of the staff met them. They presented a bouquet of long stem roses to both Tamara and Stacy. The casino needed no lights, as the smiles on both their faces would have been plenty. Michael received the two keys he requested and they went up to their adjoining rooms. Michael watched as the two surveyed their new kingdom far and wide. He looked out at the view of the city.

Tamara hugged him from behind and thanked him for everything that was being done.

"The best is yet to come," he said as he turned around and kissed her.

They decided it was best to remain hidden and ordered dinner in. Stacy, on the other hand, wanted to go out and kick up her heels for a while.

"Here Speedy, take these down the street at the casino between seven and eight o'clock tonight. You'll get ten free spins on the twenty-five thousand dollar slot machine."

She hugged them both and headed out. As the door closed, Michael inadvertently showed a moment of excitement as he put his closed fist in front of him then brought it back sharply saying, "Yes."

"Michael Canon, you're up to something, what is it?" Tamara asked with a smile.

"Ah, that means we're free for a few hours."

They finished dinner then went over the plans for tomorrow. She was so tired from it all she fell asleep in his arms on the sofa. He smiled as her champagne sat in front of her, untouched. He felt bad about turning R.C. down on having a bachelor party for him. Actually, he would share a drink at nine with him in the hotel's main lounge. He looked down at Tamara knowing life had finally dealt her a winning hand. He kissed her several times lightly on the lips then she put her arm up around his neck.

"Am I Mrs. Michael Canon yet?"

"Pretty soon."

"Listen, I want to take a long bubble bath so why don't you go down and play some games?"

He agreed.

* * * * * * * * * * * * * * * * * * * *

Half the Ranger team was there when he got to the lounge. Hugs went around and another drink order was placed. They couldn't have been happier for Michael. R.C. stood up and everyone got quiet.

"Michael, to say you haven't made all our lives interesting would be quite an understatement. You've taken care of all of us and kept us safe even when it looked like there was no way out. We can't say enough about how you set up a memorial for those that were on the team that can only be with us in our memories. We all agreed on the gesture for them but you did that on your own, financially. Even though all our battles began as a fight for what was right, you've allowed us tremendous financial gains through it all," R.C. said, then stopped to sip his beer.

Michael and the others just smiled as he could see R.C. had been practicing this speech for days. When he began again with, "I don't want to make this a long speech…" everyone laughed and applauded. R.C. laughed also then took another sip of his beer.

"Ok you jokers calm down," R.C. said as he continued. "I guess what we're all trying to say is we couldn't be happier for you and Tamara tomorrow. We've had trouble figuring out what to give you two for a gift so we all dug deep into our seven figure bank accounts and want you two to have this small piece of our love and appreciation."

Scott handed Michael a large envelope. Inside were sixteen individual bank drafts for twenty-five thousand dollars apiece. Michael sat in disbelief. The team stood and applauded him then came to shake his hand and give hugs around.

"Guys, I am at a loss for words. Tamara and I both thank you deeply. I must say we have gone through an interesting five years, to say the least. The bond that we formed together cannot be broken. There is nothing I wouldn't do for any of you, ever," Michael said as he raised his glass. "Here is to all of you, the team and to those who have fallen."

They all toasted Michael and one another. Another round of drinks was delivered.

"When are you and Monica going to tie the knot Richard? You know she wants to," Michael said as he lit a cigar and leaned back.

"Don't you start on me son. Hell, it's getting to the point when she sees a flower she says, Wouldn't this look nice in a wedding bouquet? I went out yesterday and mowed over every damn flower I saw in the yard."

That was just the start of everyone going home with sore rib cages from laughing. Michael loved all of his guys. Several of the team were moving on and he was happy for them. The send off only lasted for an hour but it was very meaningful to them.

Once he got back to the room he took a quick shower then snuggled in close with his wife to be. They talked for about a half hour then sleep overtook them.

* * * * * * * * * * * * * * * * * * * *

They ordered room service for breakfast. A very excited Stacy joined them.

"How was your night Stacy?" Michael asked.

"Oh, you are never going to believe this. Wait until I tell you. I still can't believe it…"

"Stacy, sweetheart, calm down and let it out slowly," Tamara said in a calm voice.

"Ok, I was playing the slot machine you told me about when I looked up across the room. Well it wasn't really a room…"

"Breathe hon," Tamara said.

"I'm all right. I heard this guy singing this song and then the bells went off and…"

"His voice excited you that much?" Michael asked with a smile.

"Are you kidding, listening to him made me want to go up there and sing with him. He was gorgeous."

"What was his name?" Tamara asked.

"I'm not sure. I won the jackpot on the machine and by the time I could walk away from it he was gone. I think it was Larry something. I'm going back there tomorrow night to wait for him."

Michael just sat there with half a smile on his face. He looked over at Tamara who was looking at him and shaking her head up and down slowly.

"Michael," she said slowly and deliberately.

"No I swear…" he whispered.

"I know you and when I find out the truth, you're in big trouble."

Michael tried not to smile as they finished breakfast.

Chapter 62

The banquet room at the Conquistador was beautifully decorated in a bright yellow setting with flowers everywhere. The chairs were placed in an arc forming a mini amphitheater fit for seating two hundred people. A twenty-piece orchestra behind the curtains began tuning up at five fifteen. Some of the team offered to be ushers and began seating everyone at five thirty. Stacy would stay with Tamara just off the entrance until five minutes before showtime. Tamara was so nervous. Stacy helped her on with her jacket.

Tamara's wedding ensemble was a lavender lab style coat that was open all the way in front down to her knees. Her top was a lavish mock turtleneck fully laced to just below the waist. Her slacks were silk, also in lavender. Stacy's outfit was the same except the lace top was white. Her shoes were opened toed satin with two inch heels. They both couldn't have looked more beautiful. The clock was telling them it was time to go.

At exactly six o'clock Michael and R.C walked down and took their places. Stacy came down the aisle and found her place. Monica and Marsha were already wiping their eyes. Michael looked with pride at the turnout of friends and many of the employees. He could see Doctor Wallace and his wife sitting with Doctor Ambler. Jon Erickson and Clayton Sommers nodded their heads as he looked at them.

The orchestra began playing the traditional song for the entering bride. The lights dimmed very slowly. A soft spotlight quietly lit the entrance curtains that were being parted. Tamara slowly walked through the opening, stopped for a moment, and then preceded to walk slowly to

Michael. Handkerchiefs and tissues came out from everyone as they gazed at the miracle that God had enacted. Her smile told it all as her eyes never left Michael's. It was a tremendous effort for Michael, Stacy, and R.C. to remain composed as they too wiped their eyes. Michael extended his hand and she took it. She stopped next to him and was very nervous. The minister had to wait for everyone to be seated and quiet prevailed. Michael gave her a tissue out of sight of the others.

The ceremony was one of the most beautiful ever witnessed by those attending. With only a few words left to say, the minister stopped and backed away. The orchestra began to play as a spotlight shown, not only on Michael and Tamara but also on Larry Courier who was standing on stage in the dark. Tamara had to hold Michael's arm to keep steady, as she was so overwhelmed. At the moment Larry began to sing the words, *Because God made thee mine...* the aura within those seated exploded and soon everyone was standing. Stacy held Tamara's left hand and squeezed it. As the last word was sung, Larry held it for five seconds. As the spotlights faded, the minister waited with teary eyes a full minute before announcing them husband and wife. Michael kissed Tamara. As they turned around, the minister introduced them to all present.

It seemed an eternity to reach the entrance curtains amidst the ovation they received, but they made it. Instead of leaving, they moved towards the center of the large outer hall and waited for their friends to come out.

"Michael, I've never known such happiness. That was more beautiful then I ever could have imagined. I love you so much."

He held her for a moment then she was swarmed by Monica, Marsha, and the rest. The hotel manager was one of the first to congratulate Michael. Catherine and Kennedy were overjoyed.

"You better get used to this my good friend, I think you're next," Michael said to him as they hugged.

The reception line lasted for twenty minutes. Michael finally excused himself and walked over to a friend who had taken a seat by the front window.

"Doctor Ambler, it is so wonderful you could come. It means so much to Tamara and me."

"Michael, when you invited me I couldn't have been more honored. Pardon an old man for wiping his eyes but I've never been so moved."

Tamara soon walked over, hugged the doctor and kissed him on the cheek.

"One day we need to talk about what has happened. This is not even in the book. I know because I wrote most of them."

Saying they would see him shortly, they met Larry coming towards them. He greeted them warmly. Michael looked at Stacy and motioned for her to come over.

"Larry, may I present Miss Stacy Saxon. Stacy, this is Larry Courier."

Her hand was shaking as they shook. He held her hand for a moment as he told her how pretty she was.

"I remember seeing you in San Francisco," Larry added. Michael and Tamara could see she was having a total meltdown when she could hardly say a word. Saying he hated to leave but he had to be somewhere in a few minutes he hugged Tamara, shook Michael's hand again, then gave Stacy a little hug. She was frozen in the carpet as they watched him walk away. Michael and Tamara just smiled as they got her to walk outside in the fresh air with them. As Michael lit a cigarette she finally spoke.

"That's the guy I told you about, is he gorgeous or what?" Stacy said then headed back in.

They chuckled at her and then headed in for dinner.

Half of the guests had departed; the remaining eighty-five were seating themselves around large round tables that replaced the original seating. Doctor Ambler, Marsha, R.C., Monica, and Stacy sat with Michael and Tamara. There was one vacant seat which was soon taken by Larry Courier. Stacy squirmed in her chair as Larry sat next to her.

"I understand you won the twenty-five thousand dollar slot last night?"

That's all it took to bring her back out of the clouds. She began talking about how she got there and saw him on the stage. Michael kissed Tamara and they smiled as they glanced back at them from time to time. Talk of the islands right up until now filled the dinner conversation.

With dinner and dessert over, Michael just sat back to enjoy what was going to happen next. Larry excused himself and went back stage. Stacy slid over next to Tamara. They talked for a moment then Stacy went to the ladies room.

"She is so relaxed now," Tamara told Michael. "That was sweet of you to arrange all this. Now I know why you were smiling in the room."

"Not yet."

"Michael, just looking at the two of you makes me feel young again. I am so taken with everything that's happened," Doctor Ambler said.

"It wouldn't have been right if you hadn't come down. Oh, I meant to call you about a certain matter. I don't remember receiving anything from you for your trip to San Francisco."

"Michael, sometimes my actions are dictated by my heart. Seeing the love you two had, and still do, won't allow me to ever think about something like that."

Michael thanked him and shook his hand.

R.C. started one of several heartfelt toasts to the newlyweds. It meant a lot to both of them as they raised their glasses after each toast. Stacy came back and looked a little calmer.

"Stacy, I haven't gotten to tell you how beautiful you look," Michael said. "It's a good thing Tamara went through with this or you'd be sitting one seat closer."

"Thank you Michael."

The lights blinked several times in the room then began to dim slightly. Larry came out on stage and received a round of applause. He gave a toast to Michael and Tamara.

"I would like to sing a song especially to them."

The orchestra began and Larry performed, *The most wonderful night of the year* in its entire dynamic vibrato. Chills again cascaded through them all. The applause lasted nearly a minute.

"I hope you will all enjoy what I'm about to do next. When I'm around wonderful people like Michael and Tamara and yourselves I want to do more. There was a hat…oh, here it is. Inside this hat are the names of all the women here with us. I'm going to draw out one name. One of my favorite things is singing with someone from the audience right up here on stage. To make it a little more fun, the person chosen will have the option of sitting here on this stool and letting me serenade her or join me in a duet."

Oo's and a little laughter broke out amongst everybody.

"If your name is called and you don't want to come up, we'll draw again. Trust me, this is fun."

Michael and Tamara watched Stacy starting to bite her fingernails, as she looked at all the women in the room. Tamara put her hand on her shoulder. Larry mixed all the slips up and drew one. A drum roll was given by the orchestra's drummer.

"Stacy Saxon would you like to come up here?"

Stacy yelled out and put her hands on her mouth. Michael smiled as Stacy got a nice hand from everybody. She hugged Tamara then stopped next to Michael.

"Don't look at us. Look him right in the eye and sing to him. He would like that," Michael advised.

Everyone applauded as Stacy headed for the stage. Larry talked to her for a moment. Tamara looked at Michael and smiled.

"Ok everybody, she says she wants to do a duet with me. Let me lead into this by giving thanks to Diana and Lionel for making this song one of my favorites, I hope it's one of yours too. Oh, I'll sing the first line then she says she'll come in."

He clipped a mini microphone on Stacy's collar as everyone laughed. The orchestra began the introduction of the song, *Endless Love*. Tamara kissed Michael's hand as she backed into his arms. Larry held both of Stacy's hands as he began singing the first line. Chills went through everyone as Stacy sang the second part by herself and Larry couldn't believe what he was hearing. They harmonized the third part as if they had been practicing for a long time together. Tamara began to cry and Michael was choking up from pride as they watched the two perform as one. Larry and Stacy's eyes never left one another's as the ending came to a high peak and they both held it. Everybody was on their feet and applauded as Larry gave her a hug then a small kiss. He walked her back to the table. Larry winked at Michael.

Everyone at the table hugged her as she got to her chair. Stacy's eyes were wet with joy as Tamara held her for a moment before Larry made her take a bow. Larry sang one more song, and then the entertainment portion was over. He received a wonderful ovation as he came down to Michael's table and shook hands. Larry said he couldn't remember when he had a better time. He took his handkerchief from his inside jacket pocket and touched a tear on Stacy's cheek.

"Stacy, you were wonderful, where did you learn to sing like that?"

"I just love to sing. Thank you for holding on to me. I was so nervous."

"It didn't seem like it. Your soft hands were so still it was easy for me to sing, only to you."

Larry hugged Stacy and he held her for a moment. "I don't know what you have planned for later but why don't you come down to the Sierra and maybe after my show we could have some coffee or something?"

"I think I'd like that."

Larry thanked Michael again and then kissed the bride. Michael and Tamara stood and said goodnight to everyone.

"Why do I feel every name in that hat said Stacy Saxon on it? You set that entire thing up, didn't you Michael?" she asked as he put his arms around her.

"Am I good or what?" he answered laughingly as they headed for the elevator.

They went up to the top floor. As the elevator doors opened Tamara said this wasn't their floor.

"R.C. came by earlier and asked to put something of theirs in our room until later. He returned with a big smile on his face. Now I just wonder what they were up to."

She laughed at the speculation.

Michael unlocked the double doors of the honeymoon suite.

"I think this is where I'm supposed to carry you over the threshold."

Tamara's smile beamed as she put her arm around his neck. He lifted her and then walked into the room. She kissed him very passionately before he put her down. The suite was spacious and beautifully decorated. She headed for the patio. Michael dimmed some lights then walked out and put his arms around her.

The lights of the city were breathtaking. In a few minutes they walked back inside and turned most of the lights off. Tamara walked into the bedroom as he took off his coat. She asked him to come in there for a moment. She was standing facing away from him as he put his hands on her shoulders and kissed her neck.

"Michael."

"Yes."

"Undress me."

Please turn the page for a special preview of

UNKNOWN ALLIANCE

This is the forth book in E.H. Clark's all new Michael Canon adventures.

Excerpt from Unknown Alliance

"I don't know what I did to deserve you my darling?" Brad said as Charlene rolled off of him.

"I am the best aide you could ever have. You just lay there and finish your drink.

Bradley eyes were very heavy. Within a minute he was unconscious. Charlene pulled her cell phone from her purse and keyed in a number. "He's ready."

Charlene was fully dressed when a light knock came from the door. She looked out the sight glass, then opened it.

A tall bearded man came in and closed the door.

"How long has he been out?" the man asked as he put surgical gloves on.

"Six minutes. How long will this take?"

"Don't worry yourself. Just have him in his car within twenty minutes. Nothing else concerns you," he answered.

The man removed a small bottle from his coat pocket and put a syringe into it. He had her separate his first and second toes on his right foot. Inserting the small needle just under the skin he induced the liquid slowly.

"I don't like this," Charlene said as she looked up at Brad.

"You're being paid well, you don't have to like it. Wake him up when I leave."

The man let himself out as Charlene went into the bathroom and soaked a washcloth with cold water. She returned to the bed and began rubbing it over Brads face and neck. In less than a minute he awoke.

"Boy, I can't believe I fell asleep. How about coming back in here?"

"No, we can't. I have to get going. You need to get ready so we can leave. I'll make it up to you. How about tomorrow night?"

She looked at her watch as Brad got dressed. He wanted to take a shower but she talked him out of it. He kissed her one last time in the elevator then went in separate directions when they reached the lobby. Bradley walked out to his limo and drove off.

Charlene felt empty as she watched Brad's limo leave the hotel. Traffic was light at that time of the night. A single figure sat in a car with the motor running midway down the block from the hotel. Charlene, not content with waiting for the light to change, started walking across the street. As she approached the centerline the man in the car pressed hard on the accelerator pedal. Charlene glanced once at the oncoming vehicle then looked away to her right for a moment. When she looked back to her left the car was right on her. The vehicles impact sent her onto the hood and into the windshield. The car turned the corner sharply, causing Charlene to fall hard to the pavement. The vehicle would later be found on the tide flats burned up.

"Jerold, stop someplace and get me a newspaper," Bradley said.

The driver pulled into a service mart and went inside. Brad sat looking at a file he had in his briefcase when a sharp pain shot through his upper body. The papers dropped to the floor as his hands clutched his chest. He could feel his temperature increasing as he tried to remove his coat. This effort stopped as he grabbed his chest again, one last time.

About the Author

A Pacific Northwest native and an ex-Navy man, his home is now in Minnesota with his wonderful wife, Phyllis. He's a new writer bringing into play situations that allow the reader an opportunity to reach deep within them, in fiction, to rekindle feelings and hidden emotions lost in the times. He's an avid golfer and thrives on competition. His spontaneous sense of humor keeps everyone around him very loose. A mechanical designer/draftsman by trade, his common sense approach to work and life makes his writings worth investigating. In 1998, while watching a movie he made a comment that he could write a better plot than that. Phyllis said, why don't you? From that moment on he began writing fiction novels that give you suspense, romance, twists, and plenty of action.

Printed in the United States
19085LVS00002B/214